BERG

Andrew Savile is the pseudonym of an award-winning crime writer who lives in Gloucestershire.

Other titles in this series:

BERGERAC AND THE FATAL WEAKNESS

BERGERAC AND THE MOVING FEVER

BERGERAC AND THE TRAITOR'S CHILD

ANDREW SAVILLE

BERGERAC
AND THE
JERSEY
ROSE

ADVENTURE
BASED ON THE BBC TV SERIES

CREATED BY
ROBERT BANKS STEWART

PENGUIN BOOKS

PENGUIN BOOKS
Published by the Penguin Group
27 Wrights Lane, London w8 5TZ, England
Viking Penguin Inc., 40 West 23rd Street, New York, New York 10010, USA
Penguin Books Australia Ltd, Ringwood, Victoria, Australia
Penguin Books Canada Ltd, 2801 John Street, Markham, Ontario, Canada L3R 1B4
Penguin Books (NZ) Ltd, 182–190 Wairau Road, Auckland 10, New Zealand
Penguin Books Ltd, Registered Offices: Harmondsworth, Middlesex, England

Published in Penguin Books 1988

Filmset in 10/12 Linotron Baskerville
by Centracet

Made and printed in Great Britain by
Richard Clay Ltd, Bungay, Suffolk

CHAPTER

I

'Did you know it's Friday the thirteenth?'

The voice had a soft, Irish accent that made the question sound like a confidence. Theodore Poolstock turned reluctantly from the view over St Catherine's Bay. A man was sprawling on one of the benches that lined the wall of the outer bailey, enjoying the October sunshine. He was probably in his forties, Poolstock thought, though it was difficult to be sure. He wore a filthy khaki greatcoat and had a can of Carlsberg Special Brew in his hand.

Poolstock nodded curtly.

'Unlucky, they say.' The man winked. 'But lucky for the favoured few.'

'Quite so.' Poolstock wondered if the man was going to mug him. Surely the police should keep this sort of riff-raff away from public places? It was intolerable. And the fellow was drinking – and flaunting the fact – at this hour of the morning. Poolstock edged away. 'Ah – good morning.'

He continued up the ramp to the barbican gate, hoping the man would not follow him.

'Better keep away from them railings,' the man advised him with a chuckle. 'It's a forty-foot drop if it's an inch. And it's Friday the thirteenth, remember.'

Involuntarily Poolstock glanced over the railings that lined the seaward side of the ramp. At this point the cliff fell sheer to the sea. He looked away.

The ramp curved up the face of the rock on which Mont Desir was built. On one side were the iron railings; on the

5

other was the ragged but still imposing outer bailey wall of the castle.

The drunk chuckled again. It was a sinister sound, and Poolstock quickened his pace. He tried to forget his unease by thinking about something else. It was over five years since he had been to Mont Desir. The ramp, he recalled, was designed so that attackers approaching the barbican would be completely exposed to the missiles of the defenders. The layout, as Poolstock had so often told parties of bored schoolchildren, was an interesting example of medieval military thinking.

Since his last visit, a turnstile had been installed in the archway of the barbican gate. The former guardroom was now a combination of tourist shop and ticket office. No one appeared to be about.

Poolstock rapped on the glass. A young man emerged from the doorway at the back of the room. He wore jeans and hadn't bothered to shave that morning. Poolstock frowned.

The man opened the sliding window. 'That'll be two quid, please. The guide's another pound, if you want it.'

'I'm not a tourist,' Poolstock said tartly. His experience with the tramp, such as it was, had unsettled him. 'My name's Poolstock. Hasn't Lady Wintersham mentioned me?'

'Can't say she has.' The attendant grinned. 'In fact I don't think she's ever mentioned *anything* to me.'

'This is most annoying.' Poolstock laid his briefcase on the turnstile. 'I am writing a biography of Lady Wintersham's grandmother, and I understood that – '

'The royal floozie?'

Poolstock coughed. 'I don't think that's an appropriate description of the Jersey Rose, young man. We should remember her for her good works, not her failings. Anyway, the point is, I was to examine the royal bedchamber tableau

6

and other relevant exhibits. Lady Wintersham said she would arrange for me to be shown round.'

'You need Mr Quenneau,' the young man said. 'He's the manager.'

'In that case, I would be obliged if you would find him for me.' Poolstock injected into his tone the chilling politeness that he had used so successfully on the Lower Fifth in their more unruly moments. 'At once.'

'OK, sunshine,' the attendant said, picking up a phone. 'Your wish is my command.'

Mr Quenneau, a slight, middle-aged man with a single, bushy eyebrow above his eyes, was far more to Poolstock's taste.

'Yes, indeed, Mr Poolstock,' he murmured. 'Lady Wintersham telephoned this morning. Graham can't have seen the message I left at the office – I do apologize.'

'Not at all.'

'We shall be honoured to give you every facility. Can I offer you a cup of coffee before you start?'

'No, thank you. Time and tide wait for no man. I should like to get down to work as soon as possible.'

'Of course.' Quenneau turned to the attendant. 'Kindly prepare a free pass for this gentleman, Graham. He may wish to return.'

'OK, boss.'

Quenneau led the way across the semi-circular barbican to the great gatehouse of the outer ward.

'We find it so difficult to get the right sort of staff these days,' he said as they passed over the wooden bridge that had replaced the drawbridge. 'They just don't care. It's a great worry.'

'I blame the parents, myself,' Poolstock said with the certainty that only a childless man is capable of. By the way, I saw a . . . a man on one of the seats on the ramp. He appeared to be in a state of advanced inebriation.'

'Oh dear.' Mr Quenneau's forehead wrinkled. 'It's so difficult. Not the sort of thing the tourists like. I'll ask Graham to pop down and have a word with him.'

Poolstock privately doubted that Graham had the necessary moral fibre to deal with the Irishman, but politeness kept him silent.

They crossed the clipped grass of the outer ward and began to climb the long, stone stairway that led to the inner bailey. Quenneau walked slowly, in deference to Poolstock's age and infirmities.

Even at this time of year, the castle attracted a respectable number of visitors. Poolstock commented on this to his companion.

'Yes, it's not bad, is it?' Quenneau said. 'In fact we've had a good year altogether. By our standards, that is. As tourist spots go, we're very much the poor relation of Mont Orgueil.'

Poolstock observed that Mont Orgueil was a much larger castle.

'It's not just that. We're in private ownership, whereas Mont Orgueil belongs to the States of Jersey. So we just haven't the same resources.'

'At least you've got the Jersey Rose.'

'True. We must count our blessings.' Quenneau nodded his head several times, as though he were counting them, one by one. 'Lady Wintersham tells me that we're going to stock your biography here. I imagine the tourists will snap it up.'

Poolstock coloured slightly. 'I haven't even written it yet. My research is still in the preliminary stages.'

'Of course.' Quenneau added, with a wistfulness that delighted Poolstock, 'I've often thought how wonderful it must be to write a book.'

8

Poolstock nodded. He had thought the same thing himself.

They passed through the vaulted tunnel of the inner ward's gatehouse, and emerged in the sun-filled courtyard beyond. The inner ward was at the highest point of the headland on which the castle stood. The ground sloped gently up to the squat, four-square keep, the oldest part of the fortifications; it had been built early in the thirteenth century when the French seizure of Normandy had put the Channel Islands into the front line of the struggle between England and France.

'The tableau is in the northern tower,' Quenneau said, 'but the exhibition and our little muniment room are in the keep. Which would you like to see first?'

'The tableau, I think. It's new since I was last here.'

The northern tower was at the far end of what had been a gun battery in the Napoleonic Wars; the Germans had subsequently sited a machine gun and an observation post there. The tower was linked to the keep by a two-storeyed range of buildings along the inside of the curtain wall. In the nineteenth century these had formed a single house, occupied by the employers of the Jersey Rose.

The royal bedchamber was on the second floor of the tower. It was a circular room, which had been divided vertically by a sheet of glass: one half was a Victorian bedroom with gothic trimmings; the other was a viewing area for visitors.

When Poolstock and Quenneau arrived, the room happened to be empty. As soon as they entered, a resonant voice began to speak: 'The Prince of Wales left Cowes on his yacht with a small and trusted retinue . . .'

Poolstock started.

'It's the soundtrack,' Quenneau explained. 'I'll turn it off.' He unlocked a cupboard in the wall and flicked a switch inside. The voice died in mid-sentence. 'The romance of the Jersey Rose,' he said dryly, 'in English and

9

French. The tape's activated by body-heat sensors. The trouble is, it invariably churns out the English version when French tourists are here, and vice versa.'

'This *is* the actual room where the Prince and Rose met?'

'Well, perhaps not *met* exactly,' Quenneau said delicately. 'But according to legend, they were in here together. Some of the furniture's believed to be original.'

Poolstock gazed at the tableau. A portly, bearded gentleman sat in a high-backed armchair by the imitation fire. A woman who was dressed as a housemaid knelt at his feet; she was apparently removing his shoes. On a table beside them was a champagne bottle in a bucket, and two glasses.

'Good period detail,' Poolstock said. 'Champagne was the Prince's favourite drink.'

Quenneau looked suitably impressed. 'Really? I'm a little vague about these things. The Channel Islands Historical Trust advised us.'

'Ah, yes. That would be Dr Godly, I imagine. She knows her stuff: one must say that for her.'

'Am I right in thinking your book is to be published to coincide with the golden jubilee of Edward College?'

Poolstock nodded. 'The governors felt it would be appropriate to commemorate our foundress in some way.'

'It's difficult to think of a better tribute than a biography,' Quenneau said. 'Is there much material?'

'In some ways there is too much,' Poolstock sighed. 'She was such an active woman, even in later life. Her philanthropic interests, quite apart from the school, would make a book in themselves.'

'It must be a daunting task.'

'I sometimes wonder if I shall ever get round to the writing itself.' His voice rose to a bleat. 'There's so much to do.'

There were hurried footsteps on the stairs. A young woman burst into the room.

'Mr Quenneau, could you come down to the office? Graham's got a bit of a problem with a tramp.'

'Oh dear.' Quenneau fumbled in his pocket and produced a bunch of keys. 'I shall have to go now, Mr Poolstock. I'll leave you the key so you can examine the tableau at close quarters if you wish. The door's at the end of the partition.'

Quenneau clattered down the stairs with the woman behind him. Left alone, Poolstock smiled grimly: he had known the tramp would be troublesome. They should ban people like that from the island.

He stared without enthusiasm at the tableau for a moment. The scene it depicted would obviously have to be a key section in the book. He rather shrank from some of the details. There were several references to what had happened in the Jersey Rose's letters, and it was all too easy to read between the lines. Poolstock frowned at the memory. Even royal liaisons necessarily had a sordid element. Whether royal or not, such things made him uncomfortable.

Still, the episode would have to be discussed in detail. Lady Wintersham had stressed the importance of this crucial passage in the life of the Jersey Rose. And Lady Wintersham's wishes could not be ignored: she was the chairman of the governors; she had made herself personally responsible for the commissioning of the book; and, last but not least, she was the granddaughter of the Jersey Rose.

He decided to make a start. He would make notes about the royal bedchamber and its furnishings – comfortably neutral facts that would surely be relevant for the book.

There was no point in staying where he was because he couldn't sit down, and he could hardly be expected to write standing up. Besides, it would be instructive to have a closer look at the tableau. He unlocked the little door and stepped into the tableau itself.

11

It was a strange sensation, like wandering on to a stage when a play was in progress. The two waxworks were remarkably lifelike. The woman had a sly glint in her eye. The Prince of Wales was smiling. Poolstock felt as though he were an intruder.

He told himself not to be silly and closed the door behind him. There was a small, wheelbacked armchair on the left of the bed. He sat down and opened his briefcase. Just as he was about to take out his notepad, two middle-aged women came into the viewing area of the room.

Poolstock was paralysed with embarrassment. At first the newcomers didn't notice him. He hoped they would leave. They were pointing at the waxwork figures and laughing. The glass partition cut out the sounds. Then one of them saw Poolstock, and drew her companion's attention to him.

They were no longer laughing. Their mouths opened and closed, reminding him of fish in an aquarium. The taller woman riffled through the guide. Both of them looked puzzled.

Suddenly he realized why: they thought he was a waxwork. The bed blocked out the lower half of his body, so all they could see was his face and an elderly tweed jacket; no doubt he looked in period, at least to an uneducated eye.

The seconds ticked away. Poolstock was sweating. He knew there was no reason why he should not move, or why he should not be here, but the embarrassment still prevented him from stirring. He had left it too late. It would have been all right if he had moved as soon as they came in.

The situation was ridiculous. If he got to his feet, it would become even more ridiculous, because the women would laugh at him. They would realize that he had been too embarrassed to move. Poolstock hated to be the butt of other people's jokes.

At last the women left. Poolstock stood up and wiped his forehead with a handkerchief. First the waxworks that made him feel an intruder, then those horrible tourists that gawped at him.

Another worry insinuated its way into his mind: perhaps they would ask Quenneau or Graham about the third waxwork. He would have to pretend that he had been so engrossed in his work that he hadn't noticed the women. Would they believe him?

He blundered towards the door, towards the relative safety of the other side of the glass partition. As he reached the bottom of the bed, he stumbled over an obstacle and fell. Fortunately the bed broke his fall. He glanced through the glass immediately, praying that no one had witnessed this second mishap.

It's Friday the thirteenth –

Just an absurd superstition, Poolstock thought. Another, equally absurd, superstition surfaced from his childhood: *Troubles always come in threes.*

It was time to take himself in hand. Poolstock stood up, straightening his jacket. He looked down to see what he had fallen over. He blinked.

There was a shoe on the carpet – an ordinary brown lace-up shoe, much scuffed and in need of polishing. It certainly belonged to the twentieth century. How on earth had it got here?

Poolstock put down his briefcase on the bed and crouched to investigate. He tried to lift the shoe, but it was unexpectedly heavy. A corner of the bedspread fell away, exposing a brown sock above it. Poolstock bent down further. A band of white flesh, sprinkled with hairs, separated the sock from a plump leg encased in tweed.

The trousers had a herring-bone pattern. Poolstock clung to this uncontroversial fact for as long as he could. He had once owned a suit made of very similar material.

A jingle was going round his head – it came from a negro spiritual that the Madrigal Society used to sing at end-of-term concerts. Something about foot-bones connected to ankle-bones, ankle-bones to leg-bones, leg-bones to thigh-bones, thigh-bones to –

It was Friday the thirteenth. Theodore Poolstock screamed.

CHAPTER
2

Kim Bergerac was trying to be alone in the world.

The music insulated her from Edward College. She had her eyes closed and headphones over her ears. Her feet were up on the desk. On the carpet beside her chair was a pile of textbooks and notes. She was meant to be revising for this afternoon's history test-question on Disraeli's foreign policy. Instead she was listening to heavy metal and itemizing the things she hated about this school.

She had been here for a month and it already felt like a lifetime. Grandad and her mother had insisted on uprooting her from the school on the mainland where she had been for the last few years. *So we can see more of you, darling.* Yuk. Kim thought she already saw more than enough of them as it was. The real reason, she reckoned, was that Edward College had more snob value than her old school.

The fees here were so high that the school was inevitably exclusive. Edward College was by no means a traditional public school: it had always catered for both boys and girls and, like Jersey itself, it had a cosmopolitan reputation; the children of the rich were educated on the same island that provided their parents with financial facilities. Nearly half the kids were foreign, sent here by parents who had an inexplicable admiration for English education. And then, of course, there was the lure of the school's precious royal connection: the Jersey Rose.

A touch on the arm made her open her eyes. Akbar Farzanah was grinning down at her. Kim removed the headphones, reducing the driving rock music to a rhythmic whisper.

'Hard at work, I see,' he said.

'Well, they call it a free period. Besides, Upperwood's always rabbiting on about letting us take control of our own lives.'

It was Upperwood's first term as headmaster. He had begun by abolishing the prefectorial system and substituting 'guidelines' for rules. Despite his progressive thinking, he had the knack of antagonizing the staff and irritating the pupils.

Akbar sat down in the room's one armchair. Like all the sixth-form boarders, Kim had her own study-bedroom.

'Do you want to go into St Helier?' he asked. 'I've got to drop off another parcel for my cousin.'

'OK. We'll get the bus. Have you got permission for this evening yet?'

Akbar shook his head. 'I'll take the note round before lunch.' He smiled at her. 'It's only a formality in this case.'

Half the female population of the school would have given a year off their lives to be on the receiving end of that smile. Akbar was astonishingly good-looking – and all the more attractive because he seemed completely unaware of the effect that he had on the opposite sex. The irony was that Kim was impervious to his romantic charms: she was fully occupied in trying to maintain a long-distance relationship with a boy at her old school. Sometimes she wondered if that was why she and Akbar had become friends: they wanted nothing but friendship from each other.

'I had another letter from my cousin today,' Akbar said abruptly. 'He says I've got to go into his business when I leave here.'

The cousin lived in Paris. He had acted as Akbar's guardian since his parents' death in a car crash.

'What exactly does he do?' Kim said.

'Import-export. Don't ask me what that means. As far as I can see, when he's not on the phone he's having four-hour lunches with fat Swiss bankers.'

'Can't you just say you don't want to?'

'It wouldn't work. He holds the purse-strings. There's no way I can get through medical school without his help.'

'You haven't got any money of your own? I thought your parents were rich.'

'So did everyone else. Until they were killed.'

Akbar's face was bleak. His father, Kim knew, had once been a provincial deputy governor in Iran. After the revolution the family had fled to England, where they owned a house and other assets. It hadn't been easy for Akbar and, after his parents died, it had become much worse.

'According to my cousin,' he said, choosing his words with care, 'my parents invested unwisely. When they died there was nothing left.'

Kim looked up quickly. 'You think he's lying?'

Akbar shrugged. 'Maybe. I can't prove anything. And, as my cousin so often reminds me, he's paying my school fees out of charity.'

Kim stood up. 'Come on. Let's go out.'

Suddenly she was ashamed. It was all very well feeling sorry for herself – but her problems were insignificant beside Akbar's.

They walked along the corridor to Akbar's room. All the study-bedrooms were in one of the modern blocks, fifty yards away from the Regency mansion that had originally housed the whole school.

Akbar picked up the parcel. Wrapped in brown paper and tied with string, it was the size of a couple of large books.

'What's in it?' Kim asked.

17

'I don't know. Just something my cousin doesn't want to trust to the post.'

On their way downstairs a husky voice behind them said: 'And where are you two sneaking off to?'

It was Rose Wintersham. She was standing in the doorway of Chris Gunter's room.

'We're going into St Helier,' Kim said.

Rose sniffed. 'Breaking the rules?'

'Bending the guidelines.'

Rose chuckled. She came slowly down the stairs towards them, showing her legs to best advantage. Kim felt the familiar stab of envy. Rose's figure was the sort that was supposed to drive men wild with lust; it certainly had that effect on most of the male members of the sixth form. She was as slim as a model. She never did any work; it was popularly believed that she wouldn't have got into the sixth form if it hadn't been for her mother's influence. Sexy, charming and filthy rich: the only consolation was that Rose fancied Akbar and he didn't fancy her.

'Are you doing anything this evening?' Rose said casually, batting her thick black eyelashes. 'If you like, we could find ourselves a bit of nightlife.'

She half-turned as she spoke, implicitly excluding Kim from the invitation.

'I'm going out with Kim,' Akbar said. 'Maybe some other time.'

'Maybe.' Rose shrugged, turning back to Kim. 'Anywhere interesting?'

'Just having a meal with my mum and your cousin.'

'With Marcus?' Rose smiled, but her large blue eyes were hard. 'If we're not careful, we'll end up being related.'

Kim flushed.

'We'd better go,' Akbar said quickly. 'See you later.'

They continued down the stairs. Kim was aware that

Rose was following them with her eyes. Neither of them spoke until they reached the open air.

'What did she mean about you two getting related?' Akbar said as they walked down the drive.

'My mum's been going out a lot with Marcus Wintersham.' Kim flushed again. 'There was something in the newspaper about it.'

'It's serious?'

'I don't know. You never can tell with my mum.'

'How do you feel about it?'

'About her marrying again? Not too great – but it's her life. I think she needs someone to replace Dad – she's that sort of person. Marcus seems OK. Anyway, I'm not going to be at home for much longer.'

'And your dad? What does he think?'

'*He* wouldn't mind.' Kim hesitated. 'At least, I don't think he would. When I was a kid, I used to wish they'd remarry. So we'd be one happy family again. Stupid, really: we never were a happy family. Dad always pulled one way, and Mum the other. They still do.'

'Not easy – for you, I mean.'

You could trust Akbar to see your point of view; that was one thing Kim liked about him. She had only known him for a month, yet she found herself telling him things she told no one else, even Mike, her boyfriend on the mainland.

They skirted the old house in companionable silence. There were more cars than usual outside. Among them was a large white Rolls.

'Oh God,' Kim said, walking more quickly. 'Grandad's here. I hope he doesn't want to see me.'

'They're having a governors' meeting,' Akbar said. 'I heard Upperwood talking about it to Wintersham outside the staff room. It's a special one, to discuss the jubilee.'

They reached the school gates. There was a bus stop on the other side of the road. The next bus was due in five minutes. Less than a mile away along the coast was the dramatic outline of Mont Desir. The Wintershams' manor house was even closer: its grounds separated Edward College from the castle.

The wail of a siren cut into their conversation. An ambulance flashed by, followed by a police car.

'Where are they going?' Akbar said. 'The Wintershams'?'

But the two vehicles passed the gates of the manor and continued up the hill.

Kim shielded her eyes from the sun. 'It looks like they're going to Mont Desir,' she said. 'Maybe someone's had the sense to shoot one of those damn waxworks.'

'Shall we put it to the vote?' Lady Wintersham asked. 'That the initial planning for the jubilee should be entrusted to an *ad hoc* sub-committee of three governors?'

She glanced down the table to Mr Flaveur, who hurriedly sat up and said: 'Seconded.' He was a retired lawyer, but his firm still did a lot of business for the Wintershams; he could be relied on to second anything that Lady Wintersham proposed.

The rest of the governors nodded. They were sitting in the Old Library, a pleasant room on the first floor of the Regency core of the school's buildings. The school's records and some of the more valuable books were kept here, but it was now used mainly for formal meetings.

Lady Wintersham's nephew Marcus, who as the school's bursar acted as non-voting secretary to the board of governors, made a note recording the verdict.

Lady Wintersham looked once more at Mr Flaveur.

'Ahem,' he said. 'As for the composition of the sub-committee, may I propose Lady Wintersham to serve as chairman?'

'Seconded,' said Charlie Hungerford. He was the newest of the governors, co-opted at the beginning of the term.

This was his first meeting. He had been delighted to be asked to serve as a governor. The Wintershams were Old Money. They said that association with Old Money was the best way to make New Money respectable.

'I myself would like to propose Mr Hungerford for the sub-committee,' Lady Wintersham said with a frosty smile in his direction. 'Your fund-raising expertise will be invaluable, Charles.'

'Seconded,' said the Old Edwardian whose income as a chartered accountant derived in part from advising Lady Wintersham.

'Delighted, I'm sure,' Hungerford murmured.

A rebellious clique near the bottom of the table proposed and seconded Mr Arvan as the third member of the committee. At the vote, however, sanity prevailed and Mr Flaveur was elected.

'Good,' Lady Wintersham said. She consulted the agenda. 'We come to two items submitted by Mr Arvan. First, *The Jersey Rose*.'

Mr Arvan leant forward. 'I'm not happy about Ted Poolstock doing the book,' he barked. 'He's as old as the hills, and I don't think he's up to it. His shortcomings will reflect indirectly on the school. Can't we find someone else – a real writer, someone with a bit of clout?'

Hungerford glanced at the painting that hung behind Lady Wintersham's chair. It was the Sargent portrait that showed the Jersey Rose in her fifties. Even Sargent had failed to disguise the simple fact that his sitter was grossly fat. Her face was no longer beautiful, but it had a look of sardonic intelligence.

'Theodore Poolstock is a fine scholar,' Lady Wintersham said. 'He also has a long-standing connection with the school. Thirdly, I don't propose to allow any Tom, Dick or Harry to rummage around the private records of my family. And fourthly, it's a family decision, not a school one.

Finally, I have already commissioned him to do the job, so the matter is already settled.'

Mr Arvan shrugged. He knew he would be outgunned if it came to a vote. He had no strong feeling about the biography either way, but he found it entertaining to oppose Lady Wintersham whenever possible; one had to have some sort of hobby in one's retirement.

'My other point,' he went on, 'is rather more important. I gather that Mr Upperwood's changes of policy have aroused some hostility – not only among the staff, but from the parents. Several of them have gone out of their way to have a word with me about it.'

'Headmaster?' Lady Wintersham said. 'Perhaps you would care to comment?'

Nigel Upperwood inclined his head gracefully, acknowledging the opening. He was in his early forties, a handsome man whose receding hairline had left him with an impressively lofty forehead.

'Any programme of change is likely to run into opposition, especially in the early stages.' He had a beautifully modulated voice, which he used to good effect. 'When you appointed me, we agreed on what might be called the broad strategy. Under my immediate predecessors, Edward College had become perhaps a little anachronistic. It clung to pre-war assumptions and traditions. If it's to survive into the next century the school has to become more attuned to current educational thinking. Any school has to adapt itself to contemporary needs – and this is particularly true in the private sector, where parents have direct control over where they send their children.'

'That's precisely my point,' Arvan said. 'It's the parents who are getting worried now.'

'Only a minority of them,' Upperwood said. 'And that's inevitable. If we refused to change our ways, we would eventually have to face a disgruntled majority.'

'We're trespassing on the headmaster's preserve,' Lady Wintersham interrupted. 'Strategy's our job, but we leave the tactics to him. It's up to him how he runs the school.'

'Most of the time, yes,' Mr Arvan replied, rightly assuming that the reproof was aimed at him. 'But of course the headmaster has a duty to report to us. And some matters concerning the running of the school are so important that they *have* to be referred to the governors. Allow me to take an example: a case in point is the mysterious prankster. Perhaps the headmaster would care to comment on that?'

'A prankster?' Hungerford said suddenly. 'What's all this?'

'You haven't heard, Charlie?' Arvan looked surprised. 'It's common talk in the school. Someone's playing unpleasant practical jokes on staff and pupils. It reminds me of that detective story by Dorothy Sayers. What's it called? *Gaudy Night*, that's it. I gather that the prankster dislikes the recent changes at Edward College. Certainly his – ah – activities only began this term, when Mr Upperwood joined us.'

Prompted by a glare from Lady Wintersham, Mr Flaveur came to life again. 'We have to be very careful about such allegations,' he said sternly. ' "After which" does not necessarily mean "because of which". Except, perhaps, in the sort of sensational fiction you referred to.'

'I never said it did,' Arvan snapped. 'But if something like this reaches the press, then the effect on Edward College can only be appalling. *That* is why it's a matter the governors should consider.'

'I'm not sure I agree with you,' Lady Wintersham said. 'Headmaster?'

'It's true that a few practical jokes have been reported,' Upperwood said. 'Nothing too serious. I'm quite confident that we can deal with it internally.'

'You don't think we should bring in the police?' Arvan asked. 'Discreetly, of course.'

A visible shudder ran round the other governors.

'No, I think not.' Upperwood smiled confidently round the table. 'We can deal with it internally.'

'I think we should have a vote on it, nevertheless.'

'Are you sure?' Lady Wintersham said.

'I insist.'

'Very well.'

At the vote the governors, with the single exception of Mr Arvan, unanimously supported the headmaster's decision not to call in the police at this stage. Arvan tried to get a vote on the headmaster's policies in general, but this was ruled out of order on the grounds that the internal running of the school was none of the governors' business.

The meeting soon came to an end.

Lady Wintersham smiled at the headmaster. 'I hope Mrs Upperwood is better?'

'Quite well, thank you.' Upperwood avoided Lady Wintersham's eyes. 'Virginia's looking forward to seeing you all before lunch.'

Virginia Upperwood was desperately trying to remember if she had forgotten anything.

Two sorts of sherry. Gin and tonic for Lady Wintersham, and possibly for some of the others. A wide selection of other drinks to cater for unknown tastes, like those of the new governor, Hungerford. A range of soft drinks for Mr Arvan and her husband, neither of whom touched alcohol during the day. Three trays of ice in the fridge. Nuts and biscuits for them to nibble while they drank. Two tablets of Librium for herself, now rather than after lunch. How she hated these functions.

Oh God, she'd forgotten to buy any lemons. Lady Wintersham had commented on their absence last time she came for a drink. It was the sort of comment that has an implicit criticism attached.

She almost ran into the kitchen. 'Pam!'

The fresh-faced girl looked up. Usually she worked in the school kitchens. She had been lent, grudgingly, by the school caterer for the occasion. She was polishing a row of sherry glasses and listening to Radio 1.

'Yes, Mrs Upperwood?'

'I forgot to buy any lemons.'

'There's Jif in the fridge.'

Virginia Upperwood shook her head. 'That won't do for Lady Wintersham.'

Pam giggled. Then she said: 'It's Friday, so it's fish.'

Virginia looked blank.

'So there'll be lemons up at the school kitchens. I'll nip up and get you a couple.'

'Oh, thank you.'

When she was alone, Virginia fought the urge to have another Librium. The first two didn't seem to be working. The doorbell saved her from temptation.

She went into the hall. The west wing of the original mansion had been converted into the Headmaster's House thirty years earlier. It was far too big for a couple without children. Virginia hated it: living here was like living in an antique.

Akbar Farzanah, the nice Iranian sixth former whom she had met at Nigel's last coffee evening, was on the doorstep. He smiled at her, and suddenly she felt slightly better. Virginia smiled back, with unexpected warmth. At the bottom of the steps was another boy with flaming red hair, accompanied by two girls – one of whom was Rose Wintersham.

'Sorry to bother you, Mrs Upperwood. Could I leave a note for the Headmaster? I'm going out tonight.'

'Of course.'

Their hands touched as he passed her the envelope. He really was remarkably handsome, and much more polite and less awkward than most kids of his age.

He smiled again and left. As he went down the steps, Nigel and Lady Wintersham appeared round the corner of the house, with the rest of the governing body behind them. They passed along the line of parked cars, drawn up on the gravel.

Lemons – what's keeping Pam?

Lady Wintersham stopped so abruptly that Nigel Upperwood cannoned into her. 'What on earth – ?'

She made no attempt to conceal the outrage in her voice. She pointed at her car, an elderly Aston Martin in perfect condition.

But it was no longer in perfect condition.

'See that scratch? Someone has vandalized my car.'

'Good God!' A tall governor, whom Virginia did not recognize, darted forward to examine the paintwork of a white Rolls. Someone had scratched an obscenity on the offside wing. 'Look what they've done to mine.' He had a pronounced Yorkshire accent and was, if anything, even angrier than Lady Wintersham. 'If any child of mine used a word like that, I'd wash his mouth out with sulphuric acid.'

CHAPTER
3

Barney Crozier rubbed his nose. He cleared his throat. 'Do you fancy going out for some lunch, Jim?'

Bergerac blinked. Crozier was not renowned for socializing with his underlings. An invitation to lunch was automatically suspicious.

He waved at his overflowing in-tray. 'I've only just got in. I was planning on getting a sandwich and dealing with this.'

'It can wait. And I'll buy you a sandwich. Two, if you're lucky.' Crozier lowered his voice: 'I've just been upstairs.'

Well, that explained it. Crozier didn't want to socialize: he wanted to work. In the Bureau's private slang, 'upstairs' was where senior officers lurked; 'upstairs' was a shorthand way of explaining any deviation from routine, any bizarre decision or any U-turn in policy. Acts of God emanated from upstairs.

Bergerac picked up his jacket and followed Crozier out of the building. It was warm enough for June in the autumn sunshine, and Crozier was sweating in his three-piece suit. They walked in silence to a little sandwich bar in a street off Rouge Bouillon.

At this time of year the place was almost empty. Bergerac had never been here before. It was slightly more expensive than comparable establishments in the neighbourhood, so it did not attract police patronage. He wondered if that was why Crozier had chosen it.

They ordered coffee and sandwiches at the counter. The

proprietor, a doleful Italian, gazed incuriously at them. He didn't recognize them as coppers – which was something of a rarity in St Helier. Bergerac was tempted to ask for the smoked salmon, but decided not to push his luck. Even a free tuna-fish sandwich from Barney Crozier was something to put in the memoirs.

Crozier steered them across the room to a table by the window. 'We have a problem,' he said as they sat down. 'In the words of Dr Lejeune, Michelin Man has gone to work for that great editor in the sky.'

'You mean he's dead?'

'Murdered. I'm not going to pretend I'm sorry, but I wish he'd just had a heart attack or drunk himself to death.'

As far as Crozier was concerned, Claude Yves, the freelance journalist whose excess pounds had earned him the nickname of Michelin Man, was one of the undesirable side-effects of having a free press. Yves had dedicated his life not to the pursuit of truth but to finding the means to pay for the next drink. He had been sufficiently single-minded in his aim to make a lot of enemies, Crozier among them.

'How did it happen?' Bergerac said, biting into his sandwich. Against expectation, it was excellent.

'A retired schoolmaster found the body at Mont Desir castle this morning. Lejeune won't commit himself yet, but it looks as if Yves was killed about twenty-four hours earlier.' Crozier sipped his coffee and added, 'Someone coshed him, and then suffocated him.'

'Where was the body found?'

Crozier's lips twitched. 'Under a bed in a waxwork tableau.'

'Yves was a resident,' Bergerac pointed out. 'So it's nothing to do with us.'

'Oh, isn't it?' Crozier said sourly. 'You try telling them that upstairs.'

'Are you saying that they've given the case to the Bureau?'

'Not entirely. I wish it was that simple. They want a division of responsibility between us and CID. The official reason is that the killer may have been among a party of tourists that visited Mont Desir yesterday morning.'

'So there's an unofficial reason, too?'

'They didn't spell it out. The Chief muttered something about rationalizing resources on a trial basis. Which sounds remarkably like they're planning a shotgun marriage between us and CID. Again. And guess who'll end up junior partner?'

The threat of amalgamation with CID had hung over the Bureau throughout its short history. The possibility of losing his autonomy was Crozier's recurrent nightmare.

Bergerac shrugged. 'We've survived that one before. As long as the Law and Order Committee back us – '

'You mean as long as Charlie Hungerford backs us. That's what it might come down to.'

'Well, why's he going to change his mind?'

'He might when we start asking him awkward questions. Like what was he doing yesterday morning.'

'*Charlie?* He's tied up with Yves?'

Crozier suddenly became deeply involved with his egg-mayonnaise sandwich. 'This is rather difficult,' he mumbled. 'On Wednesday night Charlie ran into Yves at Lil's Place. They had a row, and apparently Charlie threatened to kill him.'

'I get it,' Bergerac said slowly; he also understood the reason for Crozier's hesitation. 'It was that piece in the *Post*, was it? Yves' gossip item, the one that linked Debby with Marcus Wintersham?'

Crozier nodded, avoiding Bergerac's eyes. 'The real problem was that Yves insinuated that Charlie was pushing them into marriage. That Charlie stood to gain, financially

29

and politically, by having a Wintersham in the family. And Yves did it so cleverly that Charlie couldn't even sue him.'

Bergerac swallowed a mouthful of coffee. It amused him that Crozier thought he might still be sensitive about Debby. Of course he wasn't. Debby's private life was nothing to do with him any longer, and it hadn't been for years. He wouldn't give a damn if she went through a string of husbands. Just as long as she didn't get hurt. The urge to protect had outlived the other emotions of their marriage.

Business as usual.

'What exactly happened at Lil's Place?'

'Yves was drunk,' Crozier said. 'Charlie had had a few himself. They had a stand-up row before an audience that ran to three figures. Lil's bouncers had to pull them apart.'

'It's not like Charlie. Usually he looks before he leaps. I suppose he lost his rag because Debby was concerned. He's . . . he's very protective.'

There was a moment's silence. Hungerford's desire to take care of his daughter had been a factor in the break-up of her marriage to Bergerac. For the first time it occurred to Bergerac that maybe Debby didn't want to be protected by either of them.

'I want you to talk to him, Jim,' Crozier said abruptly. 'Off the record. Get an alibi off him, and make sure it's a damn good one. And don't get his back up while you're doing it. We need his support on the Committee.'

'If you want a cover-up, you can — '

'Of course I don't want a cover-up,' Crozier hissed. 'I don't believe Charlie killed Yves for one moment. But CID read the papers, too: for our own sakes, we've got to clear him. And we've got to do it so tactfully that he doesn't even realize it's happening.'

'Charlie and I aren't on the best of terms right now.'

'Why not?'

Bergerac nearly told Crozier to go to hell. But what did it matter?

'It's Kim. He and Debby wanted her to go to Edward College. I didn't, and I don't think Kim did, either. Charlie's got the money and Debby's got custody, so they won.'

'That's just a personal matter,' Crozier said dismissively. 'We're talking about the *Bureau*.'

Bergerac sighed. He didn't have quite the same stake in the survival of the Bureau as Crozier did. And Crozier's interest in that was surely personal, rather than professional. On the other hand, for Kim's sake, Bergerac couldn't afford to live in a state of open warfare with Charlie Hungerford for ever.

'All right,' he said slowly. 'I'll talk to him. But I'll do it my way, OK?'

'What does that mean?'

'It means I want a word with Debby first. She's having dinner with Kim this evening, and I might drop in. I take it I'm officially representing the Bureau on the case?'

Crozier nodded. 'I wish you the joy of liaising with CID. I've got the paperwork in my office. You'd better start by seeing the bloke who found the body.'

'The schoolmaster?'

'Retired. His name's Theodore Poolstock. And guess where he used to teach?'

'Oh, no,' Bergerac said. 'Edward College?'

Edward College surrounded her. Virginia Upperwood felt as though she were a hapless parasite, imprisoned for ever within a gigantic host body.

The only sound in the big drawing room was the ticking of the clock. The school was silent – *the beast is asleep* – wrapped in the calm of Friday afternoons. Almost everyone except the domestic staff and the office workers was in a lesson. Everyone except herself had something to do. It was true that she could do the washing-up – Pam had slipped back to the school kitchens, leaving the glasses neatly stacked on the draining board; but that required too much effort.

In the corner the television was showing a children's programme. The sound was off but the movement on the screen gave her the illusion of company. She supposed she should be feeling grateful that the sherry party for the governors had not been worse.

This time she hadn't made an absolute fool of herself. She had been lucky in that the attack on their cars had given them all something to talk about. Her mouth twitched as she remembered how furious they had been. They said that someone had walked along the cars, scraping the paintwork with the tip of a knife. Only the governors' cars, not the staff's.

The tall Yorkshireman, Hungerford, the one with a four-letter obscenity on his Rolls, had been especially upset. He had downed three whiskies in about five minutes while telling her how, if he had his way, he would put all vandals in a concentration camp and leave them to vandalize each other.

Lady Wintersham was so furious that she forgot to make any of the usual barbed comments about the quality of Virginia's hospitality.

Nigel hardly noticed her, but that was nothing new. He had always been obsessed by his job but since he got this headmastership he had even less time for her. He didn't want a wife. All he needed was an invisible housekeeper who could double up as a brilliant hostess when the job required him to entertain.

At least she hadn't been expected to give them lunch. By tradition, governors ate at high table in the school dining hall. By custom, headmasters' wives nibbled a sandwich at the kitchen table.

Virginia Upperwood bit her lip as the familiar misery welled up. She got to her feet. The Librium were in the kitchen, and so were the chocolate biscuits. She might even do the washing-up. Keep busy: that's what the doctor advised.

She went into the hall. A letter on the doormat caught her eye. She bent to pick it up. It had been delivered by hand and, to her surprise, it was not for Nigel. 'Mrs Upperwood' was typed on the envelope. There was no address.

She ran her thumb under the flap and took out the enclosure. It was a single sheet of paper. She unfolded it.

There were two ragged lines of newsprint gummed to the paper. The little black letters danced before her eyes. The message was short and very simple.

You fat old bitch. Can't keep your hands off little boys, can you?

The sign said HEARTLAND HOUSE ONLY.

The big, wrought-iron gates were open. Bergerac drove slowly up the drive, which zigzagged among clumps of rhododendrons and fuchsia bushes the size of small trees. After the shrubbery, there were a couple of paddocks, one on each side of the drive. After the paddocks the ground sloped up to a ha-ha, beyond which were the formal gardens that fronted the house.

The Triumph drifted to a halt beside an Aston Martin V8. One wing had a long scratch, recently done, because the exposed metal glinted in the sun.

On either side, the house stretched away – a long, narrow building, built of local stone; there was a central block, which was probably medieval in origin, and Victorian wings. By millionaire standards, Heartland House wasn't that big or even that impressive; but it whispered discreetly of money. Bergerac grinned to himself. Charlie Hungerford's mansion with its prominent swimming pool and manicured palm trees shouted of hard cash at the top of its voice. The Wintershams, by contrast, had been rich for several generations. They no longer needed to shout. People had already got into the habit of listening to them.

Lady Wintersham herself opened the door. She was a squat woman with a square, determined face that rarely smiled. Bergerac had seen her once or twice at big functions, where her habit of wearing the family diamonds had earned her the nickname of 'The Walking Christmas Tree'. Today, however, she wore no jewellery; she was plainly dressed in the sort of tweeds that do nothing for a woman's figure but offer lifelong protection to Force 10 gales.

She frowned at him. 'You're police, aren't you? Haven't we met?'

Bergerac nodded and showed her his warrant card. 'I understand that Mr Poolstock is here. Could I have a word with him?'

'I suppose so. He's working in the study.' She studied him carefully. 'Weren't you married to the Hungerford girl at one point?'

'That's right.'

The frown vanished: Lady Wintersham had succeeded in placing her visitor in the social network. But she didn't unbend so far as to smile. The place she had found for him was not an exalted one.

'Is Mr Poolstock OK?' Bergerac said.

She sniffed. 'He's an old man, and he's not used to finding bodies. He's also got a weak heart. I'd advise you to go easy on him.'

'I left my truncheon at home.'

He knew he had made a mistake as soon as the words were out of his mouth. Lady Wintersham looked grimly at him. Maybe she didn't have a sense of humour. Or perhaps the lower orders weren't supposed to crack jokes in the presence of their betters.

'Come this way.'

He followed her down the long hall and into one of the Victorian parts of the house. In the study an old man with very little hair sat writing at the table that dominated the room. He looked up as they entered, revealing a thin, sharp-featured face and a complexion that reminded Bergerac of dehydrated leather.

'This is Detective Sergeant Bergerac, Ted,' Lady Wintersham said. 'He wants to talk to you about this morning.'

Poolstock shrugged pettishly. 'I've told the police everything I know.'

'You talked to my colleagues in the CID, sir. I'm from the Bureau des Etrangers. I'll try not to cover too much of the same ground.'

Lady Wintersham left them alone. Poolstock did not ask Bergerac to sit down, so he wandered across the room to the window. The gardens on this side of the house were less formal than at the front. On the left was a line of outhouses that might once have been a stable block. One of them, perhaps the former coach-house, looked as if it might be inhabited. Beyond them, a stone-flagged path led to a small gate in the wall that bounded this side of the grounds. The wall, Bergerac suddenly realized, must belong to the outer ward of Mont Desir; the castle was much nearer to Heartland House than it appeared from the road.

He pulled out his notebook and turned back to Poolstock. 'I gather that you knew Mr Yves?'

'I didn't *know* him, Sergeant. We had met on one occasion. In July, I think it was. Or possibly June. He mentioned the book I'm writing in the *Post*. In many ways I could do without that kind of publicity.'

'Not in the best possible taste?' Bergerac suggested.

'Precisely.' Poolstock glanced at Bergerac with sudden

35

approval. 'The Jersey Rose is a fascinating subject, but those with a schoolboy mentality tend to ignore her virtues and her very real achievements. The foundation of Edward College, for example. They concentrate on the – ah – more lurid details of her life.'

'No doubt your book will set the record straight.'

Poolstock nodded smugly. 'Indeed I hope so. At least it should correct some of the misconceptions that have arisen about the lady. Just look at what Yves wrote. It's totally misleading. I'll find it for you.'

He began to search for the cutting among the books and the piles of paper that littered the table. His hands trembled, either from age or from the shock of finding the body. As he searched, he mumbled to himself. The chaotic state of his research materials was not a good omen for the book.

Bergerac had no desire to see the cutting. 'You noticed nothing out of place at the tableau? Nothing that struck you as odd?'

'Eh? The tableau?' Poolstock looked up, but for a few seconds his fingers continued to rummage through the papers. 'I'd never seen it before. I was only there for about five minutes. As far as I could tell, everything was just as it should be. I did notice one suspicious character lurking about. There was an Irish tramp on the ramp outside. It was only mid-morning but he was drunk. He even had the impertinence to accost me. Later, I understand, he tried to force his way into the castle.'

'I see.' Bergerac pretended to make a note. 'Tell me, when you found Yves, did you recognize him straightaway?'

The flush of righteous anger faded from Poolstock's cheeks. 'No – I found a foot first. Then – ah – I summoned help. Mr Quenneau, who's the manager, found the face on the other side of the bed. Even then, I didn't recognize him immediately. He was – ah – much changed.'

Poolstock swallowed convulsively.

'I understand.' Bergerac had seen victims of suffocation before, their eyes bloodshot and staring, and their faces discoloured by cyanosis and petechial haemorrhages. It was time to change the subject. 'It seems likely that Mr Yves was killed at some point yesterday. As a matter of form, can you tell me where you were?'

As he had hoped, the question irritated Poolstock enough to make him temporarily forget what he had seen at Mont Desir.

'Surely you can't suspect me? This is monstrous.'

'Just routine, sir. We ask everyone this question. Standard procedure.'

'Well, it's no secret where I was.' Poolstock hesitated, frowning. 'Now, where was I? I remember — I spent the morning working here. Then I caught the bus into St Helier and had lunch in that little place on the corner near the Weighbridge. I can't recall its name but it had terrible coffee. Most places do have terrible coffee these days, I find. And in the afternoon I worked in the library of the Channel Islands Historical Trust. You know it? They're in a rather nice Queen Anne house near Fort Regent.'

Bergerac nodded. He knew the museum and he also, to his cost, knew the curator. 'You'll know Dr Godly, then?'

'Indeed I do.' Poolstock looked surprised that he and Bergerac should find an acquaintance in common. He pursed his lips and added weightily: 'As a scholar, she's *quite* sound. In her way.'

As compliments went, this one didn't go very far. Bergerac's eyes strayed back to the Wintershams' private gate to Mont Desir.

'To go back to the morning,' he said. 'Did you notice anyone hanging around the house or grounds while you were here?'

'Only the family. Come to think of it, Lady Wintersham was — '

There was a tap on the door. Lady Wintersham herself poked her head into the room.

'There's a telephone call for you, Sergeant,' she announced. 'I hope the States Police don't make a habit of this.'

'I hope so, too, Lady Wintersham.'

'You can take it in the hall.'

She withdrew her head.

'I'll find you that cutting while you're on the phone,' Poolstock said. 'I know it'll interest you.'

The telephone extension in the hall was in an alcove under the stairs. A number of doors opened into the hall; several of them were ajar, and Bergerac wondered if Lady Wintersham planned to listen in.

It was Crozier on the other end.

'I've just been talking to the editor of the *Post*,' he said without preamble. 'According to him, Yves was trying to get a story out of Edward College. He'd been making a few enquiries, asking about the staff and sixth-form privileges – that sort of thing.'

'I don't see the connection,' Bergerac said.

'Maybe there isn't one. But while you're at Heartland House, there's no harm in asking Poolstock about it. You could even try Lady Wintersham, if she's about.'

'If I can. Your call hasn't made us popular here.'

'Well, remind her this is a murder investigation,' Crozier said. He throttled back his irritation. 'Tactfully, of course. She's an influential woman.'

Bergerac put down the phone and went back to the study. As soon as he opened the door, he knew that something had changed.

The old man was still sitting at the table, but he was no longer searching through his papers. His head was bowed and his shoulders were shaking.

'Mr Poolstock? Are you all right?'

38

Bergerac reached him in a couple of strides.

Poolstock looked up; he was very pale. He tapped a sheet of paper in front of him. 'This . . . this *filth*. How can they do such things?'

Bergerac glimpsed a few irregularly spaced words, cut from a sheet of newsprint and pasted on to the paper.

'Where did you find it, sir?'

'It was in one of my files. I . . . I had it at school the other day.'

Holding the paper by the top righthand corner, Bergerac slid it away from Poolstock.

The anonymous letter took the form of a four-line piece of doggerel:

> *Once there was an old fart,*
> *who wrote about an old tart.*

The last couplet suggested that Poolstock had an anatomically impossible relationship with Lady Wintersham, and that he would die before he finished the book.

'I'll take this, sir,' Bergerac said gently. 'Try not to worry about it. There are a lot of sick people around.'

'The man was right,' Poolstock muttered.

'What man?'

'The Irishman on the ramp. He kept saying it was Friday the thirteenth.'

CHAPTER
4

'We just fell about laughing, Mum. But don't tell Granddad.'

Kim put the video tape on the low table between them.

'I'm not *that* stupid,' Debby said. 'I'm surprised he lent it to you in the first place.'

Marcus Wintersham picked up the tape. '*High Society*? It's a classic. In its way.'

Kim glanced Akbar Farzanah and both of them laughed.

'Classic?' Kim said, reaching for one of the chocolates that the waiter had left with their coffee. 'I'd call it prehistoric. Those clothes. Those terrible songs. I played some of it at the Film Club the other evening, and the whole room was in stitches.'

'It's your Granddad's favourite film.' Debby turned away from Kim and smiled at Marcus. 'I think it gave him something to aim for when he was running someone else's scrapyard in the 1950s. Dad still plays it over and over again. He's secretly a little bit disappointed that real millionaires don't live like that. And none of the ones he meets looks a bit like Bing Crosby, let alone Grace Kelly.'

'It's a remake of *The Philadelphia Story*,' Akbar said, 'so it never gets judged on its own merits.'

Marcus nodded. 'It's not in the same class, is it? But I like the Cole Porter songs.'

He and Akbar launched into an informed discussion about films with Cole Porter soundtracks. Now the meal was over, they were sitting on the sofas in the restaurant's reception area. The dinner had been good – French provincial with a nod towards English tastebuds – and the absence of prices on the menu suggested that it had also been expensive. Kim wondered who was paying. It was hard to imagine her mother and Marcus going Dutch.

Kim sipped her coffee and listened with half an ear to the conversation. For the first time that evening she began to relax. It was always a bit iffy when you introduced friends to your parents, especially when the parent in question was your mother with a boyfriend in tow. But the evening was going very well. Though Marcus Wintersham laboured under the twin disadvantages of being Rose's cousin and the school's bursar, he could be surprisingly entertaining; he didn't mention Edward College and he had the sense not to treat Kim and Akbar as though they had just emerged from nappies. His behaviour contrasted strongly with the treatment she had received from most of her mother's previous boyfriends, who either pretended that Kim didn't exist or assumed that she had a mental age of ten.

Surreptitiously she watched her mother, who was watching Marcus as he talked. Debby, Kim guessed on the basis of long experience, was getting really serious about him. He could be a lot worse: he must be over forty, but he didn't look it. He wasn't a big man, but he had a compact, well-muscled body and a healthy tan. And he scored highly on Kim's private personality rating for her mother's male friends.

Debby glanced at her watch and looked at Kim. 'I forgot to mention,' she said casually. 'Your father said he might drop in around now, perhaps with Susan.'

'Right,' said Kim. 'Can you pass the coffee?'

Underneath the surface calm she was furious. It was typical of her mother to defer anything she found hard to handle until the very last moment. She had probably recognized the engine note of the Triumph outside; she should know what it sounded like by now.

Kim always felt uncomfortable when she was with both her parents, as though she had to try to split herself into two different people; and having Marcus and Susan here would make it even worse. *One big happy family.*

'Oh, there he is,' Debby said with simulated surprise. 'We'd better have another pot of coffee.'

She waved for the waiter. Bergerac came over to them, with Susan a pace or two behind him. Kim was surprised to see her here: she and Dad were more off than on at present; they had been ever since Bergerac moved out of Susan's house and into his own cottage. To judge by her face, Susan wasn't too keen on playing happy families, either.

Marcus and Akbar stood up. Everyone either kissed or shook hands except Kim's parents; no doubt they had had their fill of body contact in the past.

'I hear you're working on the Yves case?' Wintersham said when they were all seated.

Bergerac nodded. 'I suppose Lady Wintersham told you.'

'We saw the ambulance going up to the castle,' Kim said. 'And several police cars. Later there was a great big truck.'

'That was the Major Incident Vehicle.' He raised his eyebrows at Wintersham. 'All a bit too close to home?'

Marcus grinned. 'My aunt's furious about it. But knowing her, she'll learn to live with it. I'm awfully afraid she'll end up turning it into a tourist draw.'

'Another tableau?' Bergerac said dryly. '"The Body in the Bedroom"?'

'She said you asked her for an alibi.'

'We ask everyone that. But she didn't want to answer.'

'She was on the mainland,' Wintersham said. 'One of

those shopping trips when only Bond Street will do. I ferried her to and from the airport myself.'

'Do you mind telling me when?'

'She left mid-afternoon on Wednesday, and came back on Thursday afternoon. British Airways, I imagine. I'm afraid my own alibi isn't nearly so impressive.'

'Try me.'

'I spent Thursday morning working at home.'

'You live at Heartland House?'

'In a manner of speaking – I've converted the old coach-house and part of the stables. It was a lovely day, and I really wanted to go for a walk. In the afternoon I went into school. I was in my office the whole time, I think. My secretary would know.'

'Do you often work at home?'

Wintersham shrugged. 'One or two mornings a week, on average. When I have to concentrate – there are always interruptions at school.'

'No mysterious strangers around?'

Marcus shook his head.

'Must you always talk shop?' Debby said abruptly; she tried to make a joke of it, but it didn't sound funny.

'Sorry. Won't be a moment. Just one more thing.' Bergerac looked back to Wintersham. 'There's a private gate into the castle from Heartland House: do you know if anyone used it on Thursday?'

Debby's eyes met Susan's by accident. There was an instant of shared understanding between the two women.

'I wouldn't know, I'm afraid,' Marcus said. 'My windows don't face that way.'

'I had a look at it this afternoon. The lock's kept well-oiled.'

'*Everything's* well-oiled at Heartland House.' Marcus smiled. 'As you can imagine.'

'Who's got a key?'

43

'I'm not sure. I haven't, but there must be one in the house, probably on the rack in the kitchen. I imagine the gardener's got one too. He often borrows the castle's motor mower.'

The coffee arrived. Bergerac apologized insincerely for grilling Wintersham. The two men drifted into an animated conversation about the difficulties of maintaining old houses that had originally been designed for other purposes.

Meanwhile, Akbar and Kim chatted among themselves. Debby and Susan tried to make small talk without much success; they had only one thing in common, and neither of them wanted to talk about him.

Suddenly Debby had had enough. Her pleasure in the evening had been soured. It galled her that Bergerac was monopolizing Marcus.

'I thought you wanted to ask me something, Jim?'

'Don't mind me,' Susan said quickly. 'I'm going home. I need a good night's sleep.'

Marcus looked at his watch. 'I had no idea it was so late. Can I give you a lift, Susan?'

'No, don't bother, thanks.' The words were civil, but the tone wasn't. 'I'll find a taxi.'

'OK.' Wintersham touched Debby's arm. 'Look, why don't I take these two back? It's on my way home.'

She smiled at him, grateful for his tact. 'Are you sure?'

'Quite sure.' He stood up. 'I'll phone you tomorrow. And we're playing squash on Sunday, aren't we?'

Debby nodded. 'But let me pay the bill here.'

He grinned. 'Too late: I've already done it. Maybe next time.'

Marcus stooped and kissed her on the cheek. Susan swept up her handbag and asked the waiter to find her a taxi; she did not kiss Bergerac goodbye. A few minutes later, Bergerac and Debby were alone. They sat at opposite ends of the same sofa, in a state of armed neutrality. It was just like being married again.

'You've still got your old touch, I see,' Debby said.

'What do you mean?'

'With relationships. In case you hadn't noticed, Susan's *furious*.'

'She often is, these days,' Bergerac said. 'You don't seem too cheerful yourself. Did I break something up?'

'It's a habit you've got.'

'Debs, I can do without this, OK?'

She spread her hands. 'OK. No more nit-picking. I suppose you think that's my bad habit. What do you want to see me about? And why's it so urgent? If it's Kim and Edward College, I'll tell you right now, you're wasting your time.'

Bergerac scowled at her. 'It's not about that at all. I'm trying to do you a favour.'

'Me? That'll be the day.'

'It's Charlie, really. You heard about his bust-up with Yves?'

A slow flush spread over Debby's face. 'Come off it, Jim. You don't for one moment imagine – '

'No one's imagining anything. On Wednesday night, Charlie was threatening to kill Yves. On Thursday, Yves was murdered.'

'You actually suspect Dad?'

Bergerac shook his head. 'But we've got to go through the motions. You do see that?'

'But the whole thing's absurd. You know what Dad's like when he loses his temper.'

'Yes,' Bergerac said wryly. 'As it happens, I do.'

'Well, then. He flares up once in a blue moon, but it doesn't last. He'd have forgotten all about it by the next day. In fact I know he had. He had the most awful

45

hangover in the morning and moped around the house all day.'

'Is that an alibi?'

Her chin lifted. 'It could be.'

'I don't think he did forget and forgive. He's not the kind. Again, I should know.'

'All right, Jim. I meant he'd forgotten about killing Yves, or horsewhipping him, or whatever he said he was going to do. He's not a violent man: you know that.'

Bergerac swallowed some coffee. It was cold.

'Charlie's not usually violent,' he said at last. 'I give you that. But he can nurse a grudge. Are you telling me he hasn't got on the phone to all the editors he knows? Anyone who might have bought Yves' stuff?'

Debby rummaged through her bag for a handkerchief and blew her nose. 'He might have called in a few favours,' she admitted. 'But that's quite different. Anyway, it doesn't matter now.'

'It won't do much for his image if the news gets out. If he's got any sense he'll cancel those favours as soon as he can.'

'I expect he already has.' Debby hesitated. 'Why are you talking to me about this? Why not Dad?'

Bergerac had another mouthful of cold coffee. Debby knew him well enough to know that he was wondering how much to tell her. You couldn't live with someone for ten years without getting a pretty accurate idea of how his mind worked.

'Office politics,' he said slowly. 'At present, the Bureau doesn't want to upset Charlie unnecessarily. So I was more or less ordered to sound you out first. I'll see him about it, of course. This is just a preliminary recce, so I don't blunder off in the wrong direction.'

'That's not the only reason, is it?'

'Maybe not.' Bergerac put down the empty cup on the

table. 'I wanted to find out how you felt about it. Personal curiosity, if you like.'

'You mean – is there any truth in what Yves wrote? Of course there isn't. Dad likes Marcus – approves of him, too. But he'd never try to push me into anything. Unless I wanted to be pushed.'

'And do you?'

'Into marrying Marcus?' Debby stirred uneasily on the sofa. 'I can think of worse fates.'

'I liked him,' Bergerac said. 'I didn't expect to.'

'You thought he'd be like Auntie?' Debby said lightly. She rushed on, to cover her embarrassment: 'They aren't blood relations, you know. She was married to the brother of Marcus's father.'

'So Marcus isn't descended from the Jersey Rose?'

Debby giggled. 'Between ourselves, Dad's rather disappointed about that.'

'So it's serious, then?'

'None of your business, Jim.' Debby stood up. 'Can you get me a taxi, please?'

'Is it?'

It would, she realized, be a relief to tell someone, even Jim. She fiddled with the clasp of her handbag. 'It could be serious,' she said softly. 'I don't know about him, but it is for me.'

It was after midnight. Edward College was full of silence and shadows.

A few lamps still burned outside the main buildings. There was a light in one window of the Headmaster's House. A handful of other windows, scattered through the school and all belonging to staff accommodation, were alight.

Nothing to worry about.

The figure wore a balaclava helmet, rubber gloves, a

47

dark, roll-neck jersey and black trousers. It walked quietly across the lawn, sheltering in the shadows, to the new laboratory block to the north of the old house. The builders were two months behind schedule: the block should have been ready for use by the beginning of term.

The daylight reconnaissance paid off: there was no need to use a torch. The big glass doors at the front were locked, but at the side, away from the other buildings, was a smaller entrance that was still unprotected. The door opened without a sound.

Inside the block there was a powerful smell of sawdust and fresh paint. It was important not to hurry, to give the eyes time to adjust. The torch should only be used in an emergency. A little light filtered through the plate-glass windows on the other side of the building, probably from the lamp outside the dining hall.

The smell of paint was the best guide. It led to a large room beside the main entrance. A row of paint tins gleamed faintly in one corner.

Two tins perhaps. Gloss would be best because it was much harder to remove.

The weight of the tins told you how full they were. It was impossible to read the labels. Emulsion would be a bit of an anti-climax. In the end it was necessary to use the torch, carefully shaded, to make sure. Two 2½-litre tins should be more than enough.

Leaving the block was more hazardous than entering it had been, because each hand was carrying a heavy tin of paint. A bag would have been a good idea; maybe next time. One of the tins clattered against a metal stepladder near the side door. The noise seemed to last for ever. But nothing stirred.

Outside, the figure cut round the back of the labs and struck out across the grass towards the block that housed the new library and the sixth-form centre. It was easy going.

The door for the library was not overlooked. It was also locked, but that was no problem for someone who had keys for most of the school.

The Wintersham Library was on the first floor. It was a horrible place. Endless shelves that groaned with knowledge. Big windows. The highly polished wooden floor.

A knife blade eased the lids from the tins.

Must be careful, now. No paint on my clothes or shoes . . .

It was best to start by the windows, and work back to the door. The first achievement was to paint the same four-letter word that had been scratched on the governor's car in ragged letters along the floor.

But it took too long. There wasn't time for fancy touches.

Soon the encyclopaedias were on the floor, dripping with white gloss paint. Puddles of paint were everywhere. There were splashes on the walls and on the spines of books on the shelves.

That should do.

The figure tiptoed out of the library, down the stairs and into the night. The headmaster's light was still burning.

Nigel Upperwood was sitting up in his single bed, reading the *Times Educational Supplement*. He did most of his background reading in bed, now that Virginia had moved into another room.

He could hear her drugged snores coming faintly through the wall. He wished that Virginia would pull herself together. Quite frankly – as he had told her tonight at dinner – she was not a good advertisement for the school. A headmaster's wife, like Caesar's, should be beyond reproach. She was the worst possible wife for a man with a testing new job that involved a good deal of entertaining.

He returned to the letter in the *TES* – to one particular

49

letter that he had written himself. His name had often appeared in the *TES*; but this was the first time it had done so with the magical words, 'Headmaster, Edward College, Jersey', attached to it.

The phone on the bedside table bleeped at him. He grabbed the handset, glancing at the clock. It was 12.45.

'Doncaster here, Headmaster. Sorry to bother you at this hour.'

Doncaster was one of the sixth-form tutors. His first name, Upperwood thought, was John. Upperwood tried to make a habit of being on first-name terms with his staff. It was a source of irritation to him that so many of them persisted in addressing him, even in private, as Headmaster.

'Yes, John? What is it?'

'It's James, actually. Akbar Farzanah thinks he saw an intruder leaving the Wintersham Library a few minutes ago.'

'Do you think . . . ?'

'Well, it's more than possible,' Doncaster said. 'I thought you'd want to have a look. It could be our old friend the prankster.'

CHAPTER
5

'The trouble with CID,' Crozier said viciously, 'is that they've got more money than sense.' He folded his arms and leant against the bonnet of his car.

'Have a heart,' Bergerac said. 'They've got these toys, so of course they want to play with them.'

They were standing in the car park at the base of the ramp that led up to Mont Desir. Crozier had arrived on a flying visit – mainly, Bergerac thought, to discover if he could pick holes in what CID were doing.

Parked on the ramp itself, partly blocking the way up, was the Major Incident Vehicle, the reason for Crozier's irritation. The MIV was like an overgrown caravan that aspired to be a communications satellite. It was festooned with temporary telephone lines and radio masts. The untidy ensemble was topped by a revolving blue light. It was too big to get through the castle gateway.

'They're designed for urban locations,' Crozier went on. 'Having it here is a waste of time and taxpayers' money.'

At least the MIV helped to keep the sightseers at bay. It was another fine day – and a Saturday, too – so the spectators had turned out in force. They pressed against the cordon, staring hungrily at Mont Desir, as though they hoped to see blood dripping from the battlements.

The castle's defences made keeping them out relatively easy. Apart from the private gate from Heartland House, the only access to Mont Desir was by the ramp.

'You want to hear what they've got?' Bergerac said. 'It's not much.'

Crozier shrugged. 'So what's new? CID never tell us anything worth hearing.'

'First thing is, they reckon this is professional. One blow to knock Yves out; a quick, efficient suffocation; and they almost certainly picked the lock to get into the tableau. Quenneau – he's the manager or curator – swears the door was locked.'

'So they think Yves was actually killed in the viewing area?'

'It seems likely. At least, knocked out there. It was probably unpremeditated, and whoever did it had to get rid of the body fast.'

'That's a point in Charlie's favour,' Crozier said.

'I talked to Debby last night. She's prepared to give him an alibi for the Thursday morning.'

'Thank God for that. One less thing to worry about.' Crozier stretched like a cat in the sun. As it was the weekend, he had swapped his three-piece suit and tie for jeans and a jersey; technically, he was off-duty. 'We can be sure that Yves was killed during the morning?'

'According to Lejeune, body temperature, rigor mortis and post-mortem hypostasis all *suggest* 11 a.m., plus or minus an hour.'

'His suggestions are usually as good as other people's facts.'

'We can narrow it down a bit further: the kid in the ticket office thinks that Yves came in around 10.45. No one admits to seeing him after that.'

'Did he come by car?'

Bergerac nodded. 'CID found it in the car park. Keys were on the body.'

'Who else was around?'

'That's where we run into problems. The staff are simple

enough. There's Quenneau and a part-time secretary, who doubles up as a tour guide in the summer. They spent all morning on the accounts, so they alibi one another. They were working in a room just behind the ticket office. The door was open, so they can also alibi the kid, Graham somebody. All the other staff have been laid off for the winter, apart from a maintenance man who was off sick. So the killer was another visitor. In theory.'

Crozier grunted, accepting the qualification. In police work, few conclusions were entirely watertight; it paid to keep an open mind.

'It wasn't a busy day, being mid-week,' Bergerac went on. 'Quenneau and CID went through the ticket stubs. The two main events were a party from the Hotel de Bretagne in the morning, and a group of schoolkids in the afternoon. Otherwise, they only sold ten tickets. In the morning, Graham remembers two old couples, probably tourists, and Yves. I've talked to him, and I reckon he's pretty reliable.'

'The Hotel de Bretagne,' Crozier said, 'In theory.'

'I radioed the Bureau from the MIV. Goddard and Pettit are at the hotel now.' He glanced at Crozier. 'CID wanted that job themselves. They aren't pleased.'

'Good.'

'But there's a snag,' Bergerac said. 'The coach party for Mont Desir just assembled at the hotel. They weren't all staying there. For the price of a fiver, anyone could go.'

'I don't suppose anyone's sorted out why Yves came here in the first place?'

'CID are checking that angle. Nothing so far. Yves lived by himself in St Aubin. They say they found nothing at his flat. They're asking around, but they aren't hopeful. He was the sort of man that has a lot of contacts but no real friends.'

'So all we can do is check the hotel?'

'Not quite.' Bergerac jerked his thumb over his shoulder.

'You said yesterday that Yves was asking about Edward College. As the crow flies, the school's less than a mile away. The Jersey Rose founded the school. I did wonder . . . ?'

'Edward College is CID territory.' Crozier jingled his car keys. 'Technically. I must be off, Jim. I'm meant to be going shopping with Alice this morning. I suppose you'd better keep me posted if anything comes up. Here or . . . elsewhere.'

He climbed into his car and rolled down the window.

'Since you're over in this direction,' he went on, 'you might want to pop into the school. Kim's there, after all. You might want to have a word with the headmaster, even. As a parent, I mean, rather than as a copper.'

'CID couldn't object to that,' Bergerac said blandly.

Crozier turned the key in the ignition. 'I'd like to see them try.'

Nigel Upperwood, M.A., M.Ed., was having a bad Saturday morning.

The desecration of the Wintersham Library had been a double blow: not only was it an embarrassing and time-consuming problem in itself, but it also attacked his self-esteem by undermining his pet educational theory – that liberty for children did not lead to licence.

Together with Doncaster and another bachelor member of staff, Upperwood had spent the early hours of the morning cleaning off the worst of the paint while it was still wet. The library was now locked, and the school's maintenance men – on double pay because it was the weekend – were working to make it presentable again. The smell of white spirit would probably linger for weeks; and the *Encyclopaedia Britannica* would never be the same again.

Weary and irritable, Upperwood had been forced to cook his own breakfast, because Virginia had overslept. He had stumbled over his words during school assembly, and he had distinctly heard several titters from the part of the hall where the fifth form sat.

The next difficulty was a far from cordial meeting with Marcus Wintersham. As bursar, Wintersham was responsible for the school's buildings, among other things; and he objected strongly to using his limited budget to repair damage caused by the prankster. The prankster, Wintersham delicately implied, was Upperwood's responsibility; and the school maintenance fund was not designed to cope with the additional expense.

In any school in the private sector, the bursar was a powerful figure, since he had access to the governors and was directly responsible to them for those aspects of the school that the headmaster did not control. At Edward College, the bursar was even more influential than usual, by virtue of his relationship to the chairman of the governors. Upperwood wanted to cultivate Wintersham, not alienate him; and at present it wasn't easy.

It was 10.30 before Upperwood had time to go through the post. The secretary had opened most of it. He worked through it, scribbling instructions for replies on most of the letters. There were two personal letters that she had left for him to open, one from his bank and the other marked *Private*.

The letter from the bank informed him that he was overdrawn again. Almost certainly Virginia had been trying to combat depression by buying clothes. He would have to speak to her very sternly again.

He slit open the second letter and stiffened as he saw the irregular scraps of newsprint that composed the message.

You commie pooftah, know what your trouble is? You can't get it up. You are a failure here. Go home. We don't want you.

Upperwood crumpled the sheet of paper into a ball and threw it with sudden violence at the empty fireplace. It missed. He swore under his breath and opened the centre drawer of the desk. The box of matches, a legacy from his pipe-smoking predecessor, was right at the back.

A moment later both envelope and letter were crackling on the grate. Soon they were reduced to blackened fragments, which he ground to ash with the poker.

His secretary buzzed him on the intercom.

'There's a Dectective Sergeant Bergerac here, Headmaster. He hasn't got an appointment but he wondered if he could see you for a few minutes.'

'Bergerac? Haven't we got a sixth former by that name?'

'Kim Bergerac. This is her father.'

In a fee-paying school, parents were important people; you couldn't afford to make a habit of being out to them. And Kim Bergerac was the granddaughter of a governor as well.

'You'd better send him in.' He glanced at his desk diary. 'But I can only spare him a moment. I'm seeing Rose Wintersham at eleven.'

He just had time to consult his file on Kim Bergerac, who he thought was probably a dim, plain girl with a good deal of puppy fat. He noted with interest that she had only been here since the beginning of term, and that Hungerford paid her fees.

Then his visitor arrived. Bergerac was a tall, lean man with an uncomfortably firm handshake.

'Kim is in school this morning,' Upperwood said with a smile that took the edge off the words. 'I'm afraid it won't be possible for you to see her until after lunch.'

'I wanted a word with you, Mr Upperwood.'

'She's getting on splendidly,' Upperwood said. 'She's adjusting very fast to her new environment. We've initiated a Sixth Form Assembly this term, which helps to make new arrivals feel part of the place right away. You see, they're immediately involved in deciding how the place should be run.'

Bergerac looked blankly at him. 'I hope you don't regret that. She can't even run her own bedroom.'

'We believe very strongly that the best way to make people responsible is to give them responsibilities. And it's not just a belief. It's backed up by a very substantial body of research findings.'

'Er – is she working well?'

'It's early days academically, of course. My impression is' – Upperwood made a lightning selection of one of the half-dozen platitudes that he found so useful when discussing children with their parents – 'that she's not working to her full potential yet. But, as I say, it's early days.'

'I wouldn't say that Kim is one of the world's greatest workers.'

'There's no reason why she should be, Mr Bergerac. Here at Edward College, we believe in developing the whole person. Academic success at school is not everything. Indeed, it counts for very little as far as the average adult is concerned.' Upperwood ran his fingers through his hair and smiled deprecatorily. 'Our primary aim is not to produce a string of examination passes: it is to encourage the growth of mature individuals.'

The policeman just sat there stolidly. Upperwood glanced surreptitiously at his watch.

'Is there anything else . . . ?'

Bergerac stirred. 'There is one thing, sir.'

The 'sir', Upperwood realized instantly, marked a change of direction for the conversation. Surely the police couldn't have heard about the prankster? He leant back in his chair, feigning an ease he did not feel and resisting the urge to glance at the little pile of ash in the grate.

'You'll have heard about the murder of Claude Yves?'

Upperwood nodded, trying to conceal his relief.

'I'm working on the case. One of our sources said that Yves was showing an interest in Edward College just before he died. Does that ring any bells?'

'Not with me, Sergeant. He never approached the school formally, I can vouch for that.'

'But informally?'

Upperwood shrugged. 'Who can tell? I heard nothing about it, if he did.'

'Can you tell me what might interest a freelance journalist?'

'About the school? Well, we have our golden jubilee coming up. And – as I'm sure you know – we have a royal connection, albeit – ah – on the wrong side of the blanket.'

'That's not quite what I had in mind. I was thinking more of something that a man like Yves might construe as a scandal.'

'Dear me.' Upperwood clenched his hands under cover of the desk. 'Nothing like that. Of course, it's an open secret that some of the policies I've introduced have aroused a certain amount of controversy. But that's not exactly newsworthy, I imagine.'

Bergerac annoyed Upperwood by agreeing with him. The policeman got up to go.

'One more thing, sir. To your knowledge, has anyone at Edward College received an anonymous letter lately?'

Upperwood opened the door for his visitor. Rose Wintersham was already waiting in the secretary's office.

'Not that I've heard of, Sergeant,' he said coldly. 'But perhaps that's not surprising. If someone has a grudge here, we encourage them to talk about it. Openness is always the best policy, don't you think?'

Detective Constable Pettit ushered in the fourth person who admitted to having visited Mont Desir on Thursday. This one looked like an elderly sheep in a double-breasted blazer. He was staying at the Hotel de Bretagne.

DC Goddard consulted the list in front of him. 'It's Mr Jones, isn't it? Do sit down.'

The list was disappointingly short. The tour company had not kept a record of names. Several of the Bretagne's guests who were on the list had already left the island.

The sheep sank into a chair. 'I don't think I'll be able to help,' he bleated. 'I didn't talk to anyone on the coach. Once we were at the castle, I simply hadn't time for chatter.'

'Time? Sorry – I don't quite follow.'

'It's my hobby,' the sheep explained. 'I've always liked history, you know, even as a child.'

'Did you notice a – '

'And now I photograph military architecture. Mainly medieval, but I'm prepared to stretch a point in some cases. Jersey's particularly interesting because of the almost continuous military use of medieval castles, right up to the last war.'

Goddard abandoned tact. 'Do you recognize this man?' He slid a photograph of Yves across the desk.

The sheep glanced incuriously at it. 'No,' he said simply. 'It was a perfect day for photography. Autumn sunshine gives some marvellous shadows. Do you know, I shot three reels of film at Mont Desir alone. I use an old Zeiss Ikon with 120 film. It's a bit fiddly to operate – all the settings have to be done manually – but the lens is *wonderful*.'

'Three reels – ' Pettit began.

Simultaneously Goddard snapped: 'Have you developed them yet?'

The sheep peered in bewilderment at the two policemen. 'No,' he said. 'Should I have done?'

Rose Wintersham sat down and crossed her legs. Upperwood swallowed.

One of his reforms as headmaster had been to allow

members of the sixth and fifth forms to wear their own clothes at all times. Rose wore a short blue dress with a full skirt. The colour matched her eyes, and the hemline was almost certainly higher above the knee than the dress code's guidelines recommended. Upperwood decided not to make an issue of it; the matter was too petty. And she looked remarkably – well – attractive as she was.

'Have you had a good week, Rose?' he asked.

'Fine, thank you, sir.'

'And what have you been doing?'

'I'm on the committee of the Film Club now. And I made a speech in the Sixth Form Assembly.'

'Really?' He beamed at her. 'What about?'

'In favour of sixth formers being allowed to have their own TVs in their rooms.'

Upperwood nodded. 'I can see the argument.' One must always encourage youthful ideas, never dismiss them out of hand. 'If you make an official recommendation, I shall consider it very seriously.'

There was a short, but uncomfortable silence.

He cleared his throat. 'You don't object to our little weekly sessions, I hope?'

'No, sir. Of course not.'

'Your mother felt they might be appropriate after the little difficulties last year.'

'I'm through all that, now.'

'Good. The psychiatrist's report was very encouraging. And how's the work going?'

Rose shrugged. 'OK.'

'Your form tutor wondered if you might benefit from a little extra coaching.' Upperwood hesitated. In fact the form tutor, James Doncaster, had said that the only way to get knowledge into Rose Wintersham was to beat it into her. 'What do you think?'

'I don't think so, sir.' She moistened her lips with the tip of a very pink tongue. 'Exams aren't really my thing. I think I could contribute better in other ways.'

She was parrotting back his own philosophy, so it was difficult to argue convincingly against what she said. Upperwood gave it a try.

'In later life you may find it useful to have a few qualifications.'

She shook her head.

Upperwood frowned. 'Why not?'

'I'm never going to have to work, sir.' She smiled lazily at him. 'I'm going to be rich.'

CHAPTER
6

'I saw your dad this morning,' Rose Wintersham said. 'I didn't know he was a copper.'

They were standing in the queue for lunch. Chris Gunter was just behind them. He was rarely far away from Rose.

Kim picked up a bowl of soup and put it on her tray. She guessed that Chris was listening. She had never actually concealed her father's occupation, but she hadn't gone out of her way to publicize it, either.

'What was he doing here?' she said casually.

'Seeing Upperwood.'

'He never told me he was coming.'

'Maybe he didn't want you to know.'

'He's not like that,' Kim said.

'He's a pig?' Chris interrupted. 'You never told us that.'

She swung round. 'He's a *policeman*, OK?'

Chris shrugged, as if to say that the name didn't matter. He was a big American, well over six feet tall and broad to match, with flaming red hair. His parents owned a marina in Miami, but his political opinions were the same colour as his hair.

'Anything wrong with that?' Kim said, flushing.

'Bit embarrassing for you, isn't it? I mean, British cops are going the same way as ours. It's what you'd expect: I guess a job like that attracts guys with a certain mentality.'

The queue shuffled forward a few feet. Kim moved with it, using the opportunity to turn away from Chris. She didn't want to get involved in this sort of conversation: it could only lead to trouble.

But Rose said, 'What do you mean, Chris?'

'Fascist lackeys,' Chris drawled.

'Better than red robots,' Kim snapped.

That earned a patronizing smile.

'A lot of them,' Chris went on, 'are, like, you know, institutionalized sadists.'

Kim's control broke. She put down the tray. Then she picked up the soup bowl and upturned it over Chris. The soup was hot and he shouted with shock. The bowl clattered on the floor and smashed.

The dining hall was suddenly and unnaturally quiet. At the same instant, the majority of 300-odd people stopped eating and talking. Kim left the queue and walked slowly to the door.

Beginning with Yves, DC Wilson said with his usual elephantine humour, this case was turning into a series of dead ends.

Bergerac didn't bother to smile. He brushed past Wilson and made for his desk. It was just after midday.

He'd made three visits this morning – to Mont Desir, Edward College and Charlie Hungerford's house – and none of them had been exactly productive. The visit to Hungerford was one for the record, in case CID started checking up on his alibi for Yves' death. Bergerac made only a token effort to be diplomatic, and Hungerford had been predictably outraged that the police should even think of suspecting him.

Peggy, who was on duty this Saturday, was sorting through the internal mail.

'A few for you,' she said as he passed her desk.

He took the bundle and flicked through it. Forensic's report on the anonymous letter that Poolstock had received

63

was pretty well negative. Paper and envelope came from Woolworth's. The newsprint had been cut from the *Jersey Evening Post*. The sender used gloves. The envelope was addressed in block capitals. The sample was too small to be useful for analysis, and no doubt the writer had disguised his or her hand. Well, so what? It was unlikely that the letter had anything to do with the Yves case. A hothouse society like Edward College was a perfect breeding ground for poison-pen letters. The report might as well be passed to CID.

There was also a bunch of memos. The caterer requested officers not to stub out their cigarettes in mugs, but to use the ashtrays provided. The Social Committee was trying to drum up support for a Hallowe'en disco. The Met. had informed the States Police that hard porn might be reaching London from the Continent via Jersey; the Chief wanted all officers to take note. Barney Crozier had revised the Bureau's rota for the graveyard shift.

Bergerac tossed the memos at the waste-paper basket. His aim was poor: he missed the basket and nearly hit Willy Pettit, who was bounding across the office like a small, enthusiastic terrier.

'Jim, take a look at these.' Pettit dropped a large envelope on the desk.

Bergerac pulled up the flap and pulled out a thick stack of 8" by 6" prints. There must have been close on fifty of them.

'One of the people from the Bretagne was a camera buff,' Pettit said. 'Everyone else we traced just bought postcards.'

'How did you find a technician so fast? And on a Saturday?'

Pettit grinned smugly. 'I developed them myself. Luckily the bloke knows his way around a camera, and he was using 120 film: the quality's good.'

Bergerac worked his way through the photographs. The

quality was fine but the content was disappointing. The camera buff wasn't interested in people: he liked architectural detail. All of the shots had been taken outdoors.

He made a separate pile of the few that might be useful. There was a bird's-eye view from the top of the keep, showing half a dozen foreshortened tourists beneath. A shot of the inner bailey's wall-walk included the rear view of a man with a big, aluminium-covered camera case slung over his right shoulder. An elderly couple had been captured face-on, poring over the ruins of the chapel.

'There's one more you'll want,' Pettit said. He was looking over Bergerac's shoulder. 'I think it's at the bottom.'

The shot in question was a view from the bottom of the ramp. Technically it was an excellent picture: the curving wall on the left and the iron railing on the right channelled the eye up to the gateway at the top. Two or three dozen people were strung out along the length of the ramp, climbing upwards with their backs to the camera.

'It was the second one he took,' Pettit said. 'It was when they were going into the castle.'

'I guessed that, Willy,' Bergerac said mildly. Pettit apparently laboured under the delusion that no one except himself was capable of noticing the obvious. 'Get me Peggy's magnifying glass, will you?'

He bent over the photograph. A glass wasn't really necessary: a naked eye was enough. A third of the way up the ramp, two men had their faces in profile to the camera. The first, who wore a khaki-coloured coat, was sitting on one of the iron benches that were scattered along the line of the wall; it looked as if he was beckoning the other man. You could just make out a lager can on the edge of the bench.

The second man was the one with the big camera case

65

over his shoulder. He was a middle-aged man with heavy features and the build of a bull.

'Well?' Pettit was back at Bergerac's shoulder. 'What do you think?'

Bergerac took the glass and examined the two faces.

'There's no doubt about it,' he said at last.

'No doubt about *what*?'

'I know for certain who one of them is.'

Pettit was almost vibrating with impatience. 'What about the other?'

'Not so sure about him.' Bergerac hesitated. It would be good to let Pettit dangle for a little longer: Willy wanted to go too far too fast. 'I'll let you know if it checks out.'

Lady Wintersham chewed the lettuce leaf as though it were tough stewing steak. Her nanny had brought her up to chew each mouthful twenty times; and the habit, like so much of her past, had remained with her all her life.

She swallowed. 'Are you serious about the Hungerford girl?'

The question came out of the blue. Marcus looked up. He was sitting at the far end of the long mahogany table that dominated the dining room at Heartland House. Thirty years ago, a family Saturday luncheon had become traditional for all the Wintershams on Jersey. Now most of the Wintershams were gone, but the tradition lingered on.

For a moment, he looked thoughtfully at his aunt. He covered the delay by taking a sip of Perrier water.

'You don't mind my asking, do you?' she said brusquely. 'Naturally I'm interested.'

He smiled at her. 'Of course I don't mind. And yes, I think I am getting serious about Debby.'

Lady Wintersham grunted. 'I thought so.'

'You approve?'

66

'Doesn't matter if I do or don't.' She grinned unexpectedly at him; few people outside her immediate family saw that grin. 'It's your business.'

'I answered your question,' Marcus said. 'So . . . ?'

The silence lasted for a few seconds. Despite the Indian summer outside, logs crackled in the fireplace; the dining room faced north and Lady Wintersham felt the cold.

Then she nodded; she was essentially a fair-minded woman. 'All right. Nothing much wrong with the girl herself. She's presentable even now, and we can soon smooth away any rough edges. I don't mind the divorce, though the daughter's a bit of a problem. She's not too old for children, if you want them, and I like the fact she's not a pauper.' Marcus tried to interrupt but she overrode him. 'Yes, I know you don't need the money, but it all helps. The only serious difficulty would be that dreadful father of hers.'

'I wouldn't be marrying him.'

'I know, dear. But we'd have to take him up – properly, I mean – or else people would talk.' She dabbed her lips with a napkin, as though wiping away the taste of Charlie Hungerford.

'We've taken him up already. He's coming to dinner tonight, remember?'

'That's not the same. It's school business – not a social occasion.' She sighed with mock exasperation. 'You know quite well what I mean.'

Marcus did. In her own peculiar way, his aunt was far too well-bred ever to put her meaning into words. If she had, the words would have been 'a little vulgar, perhaps', 'rather ostentatious' or 'not quite our type of person'. All the verdicts were equally damning.

'You know what your trouble is?' Marcus said with a smile. 'You're an old-fashioned snob. Charlie's "in trade".'

'Nonsense, dear.'

'My grandfather was in trade. If they hadn't nationalized the coal industry, I'd probably be running a mine or something.'

'That's quite different. Ring the bell, would you?'

The Portuguese maid-servant came in to remove their plates and serve the pudding. The cook was Portuguese, too; and her excellence was one reason why Marcus did not object to helping to perpetuate the tradition of the Wintersham Saturday luncheon.

The maid also brought a letter. Lady Wintersham took it from the salver and opened it with the accompanying paperknife. As Marcus was being served, she skimmed through the contents. He glanced up the table. Her face was impassive. As he watched, she crumpled letter and envelope into a ball and threw it on the fire.

'We'll have our coffee in the drawing room, Rosa,' she said.

None of the sixth-form study-bedrooms had doors that locked. Locks and bolts used to be against the rules; now they were against the guidelines.

That was convenient. The prankster's second destination was Chris Gunter's room. The window was closed.

It was a brilliant idea for a smokescreen. Too good a chance to miss.

There was little risk of a witness. At this time of the afternoon the sixth-form block was deserted. People were playing in, or watching, school matches; they were doing the community service that Upperwood was so fond of; or they had sloped off to St Helier for a bit of fun.

The bed? Maybe the stereo system? Or why not both?

The petrol came from the tank of one of the day-boy sixth-formers' motor bikes. It had been easy to siphon it off into a couple of milk bottles, though the taste was foul.

One bottle for the bed; the other for the stereo system.

There was enough left over to saturate the miniature TV that was hidden behind the books on the shelf beside the desk; and enough to lay two trails that came together by the door.

The prankster lit a match and dropped it on the floor. Two tongues of blue-tipped flame ran across the carpet. It would be tempting fate to wait and see what happened.

The door closed softly. A few minutes later, tendrils of thick, black smoke oozed through the crack between the door and its frame. There was a draught in the corridor, and the tendrils whipped away.

Detective Sergeant McCann slithered into the Bureau and stood just inside the door, wringing his hands. His eyes made a slow and cautious circuit of the office.

'Are you looking for someone?' Peggy asked sharply. Almost everyone put a touch of sharpness into his voice when talking to Doug McCann. It was a reflex action, like cooing to a baby.

'Um . . .' McCann gave the question a good deal of thought before finding the answer: 'Yes – Jim Bergerac.'

'He just went out to get some coffee – he won't be long.'

'I'm here,' Bergerac said in the doorway. McCann started. 'What can I do for you, Doug?'

'I've just got back from France. Took the wife and kids to Provence for a week.' McCann rubbed his nose. 'Um . . . It rained almost all the time. And the car broke down on the way back.'

Bergerac exchanged glances with Peggy. 'Sorry to hear that.'

'I only heard about Yves when I got in this morning.' McCann looked round the office again with narrowed eyes, as if suspecting there might be a mugger lurking behind the filing cabinet. 'Nasty business.'

'You know something about it?'

McCann wiped his hands on his trousers. His body was long and thin, and he gave the impression that he was made of india rubber.

'I don't know,' he said helplessly. 'I told my boss about it, and he said I should see you, as CID's liaising with the Bureau over this.' He shook his head and leant wearily against the nearest wall. 'But I'm probably wasting your time.'

'Try me and see,' Bergerac said.

It usually paid off to be patient with McCann. He ran the CID's small drug squad and to the surprise of everyone, apparently not excluding himself, had built up an excellent track record of arrests and seizures.

'I ran into Yves just before I went on leave,' McCann said. 'Friday, it must have been – yesterday week. He wanted to know if there was any truth in the rumour that there was a lot of cocaine coming into Jersey.'

'The figures for this year's seizures are already higher than last year's, aren't they?'

McCann nodded. For an instant he looked almost intelligent. 'Over 40 per cent. We haven't published the figures yet but it's an open secret.'

'Why did Yves want to know?'

'He knew it already – just wanted it confirmed. What he was really interested in was the arrest statistics. Specifically, he wanted to know if cocaine use was increasing among kids.'

'Bit out of their price range, isn't it?'

'Not so much now. The market's flooded at the moment, so the price has dropped. So far this year, 63 per cent of the arrests for possession have been teenagers.'

'What did you tell him, then?'

McCann shrugged. 'I said he might not be completely wrong. And we talked a bit more until he offered a deal. So I gave him the exact figures, off the record, of course. He could have got them elsewhere if he wanted, so there was no point in clamming up. In return, he told me that he'd heard a whisper that the Golden Ball might be a distribution centre.'

Bergerac felt a twinge of admiration for McCann. Few policemen had ever succeeded in making a reasonable deal with Yves. When Michelin Man offered to trade information, the trade was usually in one direction.

'That's a pub, isn't it?' he said.

'Up beyond Gorey. It had a facelift last year. The new management are trying to attract the under-thirties.' McCann's long face lengthened still further. 'Discos,' he added gloomily. 'Live music. Fancy-Dress Theme Evenings.'

Bergerac put down his coffee and examined the map of the island that hung on the wall near Peggy's desk. 'There it is.' He stabbed the Golden Ball with his forefinger. 'About half a mile from Edward College, and not much further from Mont Desir.'

'Um . . . That occurred to me, too.'

'Did Yves mention the school or the castle?'

'No. Have you come across anything that might be my business?'

Bergerac shook his head. 'I'll tell you if I do. I promise.'

McCann prised himself away from the wall. 'Now, where was I going?' he asked himself.

Behind him, Peggy turned a laugh into an unconvincing cough.

'Doug – did you get anything else out of Yves? Anything at all?'

McCann sucked in his cheeks and released them. He did this three times and with great deliberation, as though the movement formed part of a complex and esoteric aerobics exercise.

'We met in a bar,' he said at last. 'Yves was on the phone when I got there. I wondered if he was worried about his health, because he was trying to get hold of a doctor. He sounded rather agitated. What I actually heard him say was, "No, you can't help. I'll ring back later. I want to talk to Dr Godly."'

Kim Bergerac walked wearily up the stairs. The block was silent. There was a distant roar from Big Side, where the First XV were getting thoroughly thrashed by their opposite numbers from Victoria College.

Her shoes were stained with sea-water and sprinkled with sand. They were ruined, but Kim was past caring. She fixed her mind on a long shower and a cup of coffee.

At the top of the stairs she paused, surprised to see Mr Doncaster standing in the doorway of Chris Gunter's room; she would have expected him to be watching the match, because he coached the First XV.

The air smelled of burning plastic. She glanced past the tutor into the room. It looked as though it had been blasted simultaneously by a flame-thrower and a fire extinguisher. One of the maintenance men was standing by the window, frowning at the damage.

'What's happened, sir?'

'I want a word with you, Kim,' Doncaster said abruptly. He was a broad-shouldered young man with a rugby blue from Cambridge. 'I'll be along to your room in a moment.'

'OK.'

Kim walked along the corridor to her own room, irritated that she would have to postpone the shower. Presumably the prankster had struck again. It was all getting a bit too close to home. She opened her door. Her feet crunched on broken glass.

She stood, just inside the room, trying to register what she saw. The shock froze her mind for a few seconds. Then came the thaw.

The first thing she thought was that it was like being

72

raped. Your room was like your body: it was personal and private. Someone hated her enough to abuse it.

The carpet was a sea of feathers and down. The duvet cover was draped over the end of the bed. It had been disembowelled with a knife. The glass came from the frame that used to hold the photograph of her boyfriend. The photograph had been ripped into pieces and scattered on the bed. A single word was scrawled in felt-tip across the mirror: PIGLET.

CHAPTER
7

Charlie Hungerford wandered from room to room in the big house, listening to the sound of his own footsteps.

He hated being at home by himself at the best of times. Debby was out shopping in St Helier. The staff had the day off. He was alone, and there was nothing to fill the gap between afternoon tea, which he had had by himself in the library, and driving over to Heartland House. At least *that* was something to look forward to. The Wintershams were notoriously choosy about whom they invited to dinner.

In the meantime, however, he had nothing to fill his mind except the unpleasant memory of what had happened this morning. His aimless wandering had brought him back to the library. He stared towards the oil painting of a murky nineteenth-century seascape that hung in one corner. He wasn't looking at the picture but through it, to the safe that was embedded in the wall behind; in his mind, he saw through the door to the cheap white envelope that was lying, isolated from the rest of the safe's contents, on the top shelf.

No need to get it out. He could remember the brief message by heart. When it had arrived in the post this morning, his first impulse had been to throw it away. He had been tempted to tell Jim Bergerac about it this morning, but his ex-son-in-law had made him too angry with his absurd insinuations about Claude Yves. He couldn't very well show the letter to Debby. Not in the circumstances.

On second thoughts, he decided to hang on to it for a while. You never knew. He would make a few inquiries: it would be useful to discover if other people had received similar letters. He was torn between a dread of publicity and a desire to throttle the sender of that anonymous filth.

You dirty old goat. You screw your own daughter. That's why she lives at home. Keep it in the family.

Hungerford shivered. You could rely on no one, not even the police, to be completely discreet. It was irrelevant that the allegation was unfounded. The point was, as he knew from experience, mud had a habit of sticking; in the past he had thrown a few handfuls at other people; purely in the way of business, of course.

It was time to take himself in hand; there was nothing to be gained from brooding. He poured himself a small whisky – he didn't want to get plastered before he got to Lady Wintersham's – and switched on the television and the video. He opened the cabinet where he kept the tapes. His collection was meticulously organized: each tape had its place in Hungerford's private classification scheme; their contents were recorded in a card index.

One tape, however, was not in its proper place – it lay on its side on the front of one of the shelves. Hungerford picked it out. It was *High Society*, the tape that Kim had borrowed; presumably Debby had brought it back last night. Despite his increasingly irascible attempts to teach her, his daughter had never managed to get to grips with the classification scheme.

High Society – that was what he needed. It was guaranteed and unadulterated escapism. He pushed the tape into the video, pressed fast-forward and carried his glass and the remote-control to his chair. He knew the film so well that he now dipped into it, sampling and re-sampling favourite scenes, rather than watching it straight through from start to finish. After frequent repetition, he could judge the location of a particular scene by the tape counter.

The tape was within about thirty seconds of the magical moment when Crosby and Sinatra sang 'Well Did You Evah'. Hungerford pressed the play-button. The VCR clicked and whirred with the well-bred unobtrusiveness that is the hallmark of expensive machinery.

The TV screen filled with unexpected images. A concrete floor, spattered with drops of blood. A large metal workbench, its paintwork chipped and stained with oil. Someone was lying on top of the workbench: all you could see from this angle were two bare and dirty feet, their soles to the camera, wriggling violently. The picture was askew and trembled a little, which suggested that the camera was hand-held.

Hungerford frowned.

On the soundtrack, someone was breathing heavily – a feral, gloating sound that put Hungerford in mind of a wild animal crouching over his prey. Then a woman began to scream.

The camera angle changed. There was a naked girl strapped to the workbench. Hungerford swallowed. She must be younger than Kim, hardly in her teens. It was disgusting: it shouldn't be allowed. Her lank brown hair fanned out around her head, and the sweat glistened on her body. The skin was disfigured with burns and welts.

Without warning, both the breathing and the screams were drowned by a harsh, mechanical whine. A naked man appeared on the screen; the camera was behind him. He was carrying a chain saw.

The girl's mouth gaped even more widely, revealing yellow, irregular teeth. This time the scream almost drowned the sound of the saw. The blade touched her body.

The spell broke.

Hungerford retched as he struggled to his feet. The remote control and the glass fell to the floor. The whisky splashed his trousers. The glass shattered into fragments of crystal. He plunged at the VCR, almost knocking it off the shelf in his haste to reach the stop button.

At last the screen was blank and the room was silent.

But there was little consolation in that. Hungerford stood there, swaying with shock. No film technician in the world could have simulated what happened when the saw bit into the flesh.

'I'm sorry, Headmaster, but I can't accept that.'

Upperwood held on to his temper. Bluster wouldn't help, not with this member of staff. He would try a subtler approach, which could hardly fail to be effective with this muscle-bound teacher. James Doncaster had just managed to scrape a pass degree in geography; it went without saying that he had been appointed by the previous head-master, who made a fetish of rugby football. Nigel Upper-wood, who had a first-class honours degree, with distinction, in psychology and sociology, privately despised Doncaster for his sporting achievements. He also disliked the fact that Doncaster had held a short-service commission before becoming a schoolmaster: there was no longer a place for warmongers at Edward College.

'Look, James,' he said, leaning forward across his desk. 'Let's get this in perspective. We mustn't – '

'It's already in perspective,' Doncaster interrupted. 'We've got a loony on the loose in the school. "The Prankster" with a capital P – he's become part of the folklore.'

The long autumn twilight was creeping into the study. Upperwood decided against turning on the lights; he preferred his face to remain in shadow at the moment.

He tried again: 'But don't you agree – it's so easy to get this sort of thing out of proportion?'

Doncaster flushed at the implied criticism. 'I've made a list of what's happened since the beginning of term.' He slapped a piece of paper on the desk. 'There have been three types of incident: damage to school property, like the attack on the Wintersham Library; anonymous letters – '

'Anonymous letters?'

'I've had one. I know of one or two others, and I expect a lot of people just ripped theirs up and pretended it didn't happen.'

Doncaster's eyes met Upperwood's. The latter was the first to drop his gaze.

'And now, this afternoon,' the younger man went on, 'there's a third category: the attacks on students' rooms. It was bloody lucky I happened to smell the smoke in Gunter's room. The whole block could have gone up. And as for Kim Bergerac, she – '

'I've already interviewed them both,' Upperwood said. '*And* some of their friends.

'Rose Wintersham? Akbar Farzanah?'

Upperwood nodded. 'Among others. I gather that it's by no means certain that these last attacks were the work of the Prankster. Gunter and Kim Bergerac had some sort of quarrel at lunchtime.'

'So they each went off and vandalized the other's room?' Doncaster's face showed what he thought of the suggestion.

'Or one of them did. And then vandalized his – or her – own room to throw us off the scent. Kim claims to have spent all afternoon walking by herself along St Catherine's Bay. Gunter says he wandered around the school grounds, also by himself for most of the time. If my theory's right, Kim Bergerac is the more likely candidate, in psychological terms. Chris Gunter's a straightforward sort of boy.'

'Rubbish,' Doncaster said. 'Anyway, I don't agree that

78

the attacks on the rooms aren't connected with the other incidents. It's much more likely that the Prankster's behind everything.'

'You're perfectly entitled to your opinion.' Upperwood interlaced his fingers. 'But there is no need for you to be concerned. I'm aware of the problem, and I'm formulating a strategy to deal with it. In due course, I shall ask you and other members of staff for their views.'

Doncaster shook his head. 'We haven't time for that, Headmaster. It's not just that the school's in a ferment and the parents are beginning to talk. The kids are getting *scared*. At first they thought it was a good laugh – the Prankster seemed like Robin Hood or someone, cocking a snook at authority. But it's not like that any more. Now they're afraid that their possessions are next on the Prankster's list. Or worse.'

Upperwood looked up. 'What do you mean by that?' he said quickly.

'It's obvious, isn't it? The incidents have been escalating gradually. They're becoming more ambitious, more violent. The Prankster's got his hand in now. So he'll be moving on to the next stage – which could be attacking people, not things.'

'Oh, come now – '

'Thirty of those kids are my direct responsibility. I'm not allowing them to be put at risk. We need to get the police in, and maybe organize our own patrols.'

'Have you thought about the publicity that would entail?'

'Damn the publicity.' Doncaster stood up. 'Mr Arvan's the governor responsible for staff liaison, isn't he?'

Upperwood nodded unwillingly.

'If the police aren't involved by tomorrow, I shall be writing formally to him about this,' Doncaster said quietly. 'And I know for a fact that several of my colleagues would be willing to sign the letter.'

It was mutiny, Upperwood thought, with a rush of panic as the implications flooded into his mind. The staff were perfectly entitled, in exceptional cases, to by-pass the headmaster and appeal directly to the governors. Such a letter could seriously undermine his authority before he had time to get himself properly established. It would play into the hands of Arvan and his supporters in the anti-Upperwood camp. He couldn't even rely on Lady Wintersham's support. If the scandal developed, it could permanently destroy his position at Edward College.

There was only one thing to do – salvage as much as he could from the disaster. Doncaster had forced his hand.

'You must do as you think fit,' Upperwood said coldly. 'But perhaps I should tell you this. I'm dining with Lady Wintersham and several of the other governors this evening. I had already decided to raise the matter informally with them. I intend to call in the police tomorrow.' He sighed, hoping to convey that the cares and responsibilities of a headmaster were so vast and complex that no mere assistant master could be expected to understand them. 'Naturally, I didn't want to mention this to the staff until I had had a chance to talk to the governors. I must stress that this is in confidence, James. Between you, me and these four walls.'

He frowned, wondering if the words sounded convincing. Subtleties, unfortunately, were wasted on a person like Doncaster. The man was most unsuitable – he would have to go as soon as possible. Unfortunately he was past his probationary period, but a patient headmaster could always find a way of easing out an unwanted member of staff.

Doncaster opened the door. 'All right, Headmaster. If the police are here by tomorrow morning, I won't send that letter. Good evening.'

The door closed behind him. For a long time, Upperwood sat in the darkening study. In his mind he was setting priorities and identifying targets: first, neutralize the Prankster with the minimum of publicity; second, consolidate his position with the governors; third, get rid of that fool Doncaster.

Once those three goals were achieved, he could set about his real aim – of making Edward College, under his guidance, the most talked-about school in Great Britain. The way to do that, he believed, was to create a unique synthesis, the Upperwood Educational Ethos, between traditional values and progressive ideas. Then, once his reputation was established, he would move on to other, more prestigious schools. He drifted more and more deeply into the familiar, sustaining reverie.

Without warning, the door opened and the overhead light snapped on. He blinked at his wife, who was standing on the threshold. She was wearing a brown, sack-like dress and her hair looked as though something had been nesting in it.

'I'm busy, Virginia,' he said testily.

'I'm not coming this evening.'

'But you must. Lady Wintersham invited us both.'

She shook her head vigorously. 'I can't face it, Nigel. You can say I'm ill or something. I don't care.'

He cleared his throat. 'I don't think you realize – '

'Oh, shut up. I'm not one of your bloody fourth formers.'

The door slammed behind her.

'I know,' Dr Godly said regretfully to Detective Sergeant Bergerac. 'You don't have to spell it out. It's not my luscious body you're after, unfortunately. It's my well-stocked mind.'

Bergerac looked down at the table. They were in Odell's wine bar in Halkett Place. He had been uncomfortably conscious of Jenny Godly's body ever since she walked through the door. She was wearing a dark-blue dress that emphasized the shape of what it concealed; and it didn't conceal very much in the first place.

'I hope I've not ruined your evening,' he muttered. 'You could have come to the Bureau. It would have been less far for you to drive.'

'The Bureau? On a Saturday night?' She edged closer to him on the velvet covered bench. Her blonde hair touched his shoulder; it smelled freshly washed. 'If you want to interrogate me, the least you can do is make a social occasion of it.'

'Jenny, I can't stay long, I've – '

'You've got to rush off and arrest someone, as usual. There's no need to apologize, Jim. As a matter of fact, I've got to spend the rest of the evening writing an article on the demise of the Jersey Militia. Riveting stuff. So don't worry.'

He grinned at her, and suddenly the awkwardness between them dissolved. They had met six months earlier, when Bergerac had needed some specialized historical information for a case. Jenny Godly was the highly qualified curator of the Channel Islands Historical Trust and one of Jersey's most respected historians; she was also an alarmingly attractive woman who had taken a frank fancy to Jim Bergerac. Bergerac's awkwardness with her was due to the fact that the feeling was reciprocated; the only thing he couldn't match was her frankness.

'You mentioned Claude Yves on the phone,' she said, making it easy for him. 'What do you want to know?'

'You did know him?'

She picked up her glass of wine. 'I met him on Tuesday. He rang up and made an appointment just before the weekend.' The glass stopped halfway to her lips. Her eyes were wide with shock. ' "You *did* know him?" – what's that supposed to mean?'

'Haven't you heard? He's dead.'

Jenny lowered the glass. 'But what happened?'

'He was murdered at Mont Desir on Thursday. His body was found yesterday, and we'd like to know who did it.' He frowned at her. 'How come you didn't know? It's been headline news.'

She shrugged. 'I catch up with the contemporary world by reading the Sunday newspapers. During the rest of the week I only hear the news by accident.'

It sounded thin to him. What he felt must have shown on his face, because she went on: 'I live in the past, you know – it's my job. Anyway, 90 per cent of the news is either dull or drivel.'

'I suppose that explains it.' Bergerac added, before he could stop himself: 'I wondered why you hadn't been in touch.'

That provoked a snort of laughter from her. Jenny grasped his meaning at once. 'I see. If I'd known that Yves had been murdered, it would have given me a cast-iron excuse to give my telephonic seduction routine another try.'

'I didn't mean – '

'Never mind, Sergeant. We can all be tactless. How did you know that Yves had seen me?'

'Someone overheard him trying to reach you on the phone. What did he want?'

Her mind was already racing ahead. 'You need to know what he was doing at Mont Desir, right? Well, that's something I can tell you. I sent him there to have a look at the Jersey Rose' – her lips twitched – 'in the middle of *her* seduction routine.'

'Why was he interested in her?'

'I got the impression that in the long run he was more interested in Lady Wintersham. He tried to disguise it, but I've a feeling he was looking for dirt on her.'

'That figures. Yves wasn't a nice man – he had a

vindictive streak. So you think he wanted to get at her by digging up something discreditable about her granny?'

'Just an idea, Jim – that's all. He said he was planning a feature about the Jersey Rose. He was going to syndicate it on the mainland, maybe with a companion piece about Lily Langtry. He started off trying to lull me, by asking really stupid questions, like why did I think Edward VII chose two mistresses from Jersey.'

'What made him come to you? Are you an expert on the Jersey Rose?'

'God forbid.' Jenny swallowed the rest of her wine. 'No, it's just that Ted Poolstock has been using our library for his so-called biography, and I've looked over his shoulder once or twice. And one picks up scraps of information here and there . . . Unless I'm very wrong, that's one book that's never going to get written.'

'Why not?'

'He's not up to it. But if he does write it, it'll be rubbish. Lady Wintersham wants what you might call the Authorized Version. And what Lady Wintersham wants, she generally gets. As Yves went on, it was obvious that he knew all about Poolstock. My guess is that he wanted to get in first with a hatchet job.'

Poolstock. Bergerac had almost forgotten about him. Something the old man had said could be important; something didn't quite fit, but he couldn't for the life of him remember what it was.

He looked at his watch; he was already running late this evening. 'What's the story, then? All I know is that Rose had a fling with Edward VII when he was Prince of Wales.'

'It was in 1884, I think. Mont Desir was leased by a man called Colonel Sir Sefton Inchbald-Asprey. He converted part of the inner ward into the Victorian equivalent of a weekend cottage. He was in the Prince of Wales' set – you know, baccarat and horse-racing, all considered to be very

84

fast – and the Prince announced that he was going to pop in for a night or two on his way to the South of France. He travelled incognito in his yacht, from Cowes. The story goes that he took a fancy to Rose and had his wicked way with her. She was working as a servant there. A month or two after the visit she went to Inchbald-Asprey and told him that she was pregnant – by the Prince.'

'A bit awkward for him?'

'Exactly. He couldn't very well complain to the Prince, even if he'd wanted to. It would have been social suicide in those days. On the other hand, if the story got out, if the girl talked, the Prince would be even less pleased. So Inchbald-Asprey did the sensible thing: gave Rose a whacking great dowry and married her off to a rising young tradesman in St Helier. A jeweller.'

'Didn't anyone raise an eyebrow, even?'

'The rich could do that sort of thing. But that wasn't the end of it. Rose was financially shrewd and she made sure that her husband made a fortune. Then he conveniently died when Rose was in her forties. That's when she cashed in the royal chip. She had the decency to wait till then.'

'Wait for what?'

'Do you think I could have some more wine?' She held out her empty glass. 'Talking's thirsty work.'

Bergerac mimed a pouring motion to Robin Odell behind the bar. His own orange juice was untouched.

'It's 1904,' Jenny went on. 'Edward VII is on the throne. Rose is a rich widow with three marriageable daughters and one problem: she's labelled as trade. Shop-soiled. Not worthy to mingle with the nobs. So she plays the court card very carefully. The Inchbald-Aspreys, who were still at Mont Desir, had to accept her socially; otherwise she threatened to blow the gaff on the cover-up. Where the Inchbald-Aspreys led, the rest of Jersey followed. It was an open secret very soon but there was no scandal. All the daughters made good marriages – the eldest one, the King's bastard, married the Inchbald-Asprey son; they were Lady Wintersham's parents. Rose gave them the freehold of Mont Desir as a wedding present.'

'Very romantic,' Bergerac said.

'They never lived there – preferred Heartland House. Anyway, once the daughters were off her hands, Rose entrenched herself still further with Good Works – at one point, she was on practically every charitable committee on the island.'

She fell silent as Odell brought the drinks. He made only a token attempt to conceal his curiosity about Jenny. He had only seen Bergerac with Susan before.

'Can we speed this up?' Bergerac said when they were alone again. 'I'm in a hurry – I've got to meet someone.'

'Male or female?'

'Male. And it's work.'

'I'm work, too,' Jenny said. 'Remember? But anything to oblige. It was only near the end of her life that Rose went off the rails a bit. She produced a privately printed volume of letters, which she said were from the king. For family circulation only, but favoured outsiders were allowed to glimpse the odd page. Then she founded Edward College – technically in memory of her husband, whose name happened to be Edward; but everyone knew the real reason. So there you have it: from royal romance to civic virtue – a simple tale of Victorian self-help. You can guess how Lady Wintersham wants it told.' She paused. 'If she wants it told at all.'

'You explained all this to Yves?'

'More or less.' She dropped her eyes demurely. 'Did I mention that Lady Wintersham is one of our trustees? We get a very substantial grant from the Wintersham Foundation.'

Bergerac was becoming used to Jenny's oblique methods

of conveying information. He felt oddly disappointed in her. 'You don't want to rock the boat,' he said flatly. 'So you gave him the Authorized Version. I thought you historians were supposed to be wedded to the truth.'

'In this case we don't know the truth,' she said. 'The Authorized Version of the Jersey Rose is good for the Trust – and it's good for tourism, too. It harms no one, and it gives a lot of pleasure. If I were to point out the alternative, Lady Wintersham would almost certainly withdraw the Foundation's support from us.'

'What's the alternative?'

'Any reputable historian would tell you that the whole thing stinks. It's true that Edward stayed at Mont Desir in 1884, and it's true that Rose was pregnant with the girl who became Lady Wintersham's mother. But there's no evidence that the one thing led to the other – except Rose's word. It doesn't fit with Edward's track record – he liked to have his fun with ladies, not with the hired help. On the other hand, Rose had every reason to lie about it – it wasn't much fun being an unmarried mother in those days. The Inchbald-Aspreys would have slung her out on her ear.'

'Whereas this way she got a wedding ring and a dowry, plus whatever long-term benefits she could screw out of the royal connection?'

'It makes sense, Jim. As I said, she was a shrewd woman. And she had nothing to lose. If I'm right, you almost have to admire her: she played on their snobbery and their hypocrisy.' She grinned. 'You could say she gave them what they deserved.'

'Wait a minute. If she was lying all along, you'd think that someone would have noticed. Damn it, it's over a hundred years. That's a long time to fool everyone.'

'That's not how it works,' Jenny said. 'Time was on Rose's side, and it still is. If you keep telling a lie for long enough, people will believe it's the truth. Half of what we call history's like that.'

'But what about those letters? The ones she published?'

'What letters? They add up to a point against her. No one's ever seen the originals; Poolstock said they were lost in the war. He's seen a copy, but he's the only outsider that has. And how come Edward wrote to her? If the original story's true, he didn't even know she was pregnant. And there's no evidence that they met in later life.'

'How much of this did Yves suspect? Any ideas?'

Jenny sipped her wine, considering the question. Bergerac found her painfully beautiful when she was absorbed. They were only a few inches apart. It would have been so easy to touch her.

'I'm not sure,' she said. 'He knew about Lady Wintersham and the Trust, so he couldn't afford to be too open with me. He wasn't a fool, and I didn't tell him any lies. So in theory he could have seen the weaknesses in the Authorized Version. I think he was going to go on digging.'

'How much does it really matter?' Bergerac said, suddenly angry; his anger had nothing to do with the Jersey Rose or the Yves case.

He was dimly aware that the street door had opened.

'It matters to Lady Wintersham, all right,' Jenny said. 'In unguarded moments she's said to refer to the Queen as "My first cousin, once removed" . . . Have I helped you at all?'

He smiled at her. 'You've just made things more complicated.'

The street door closed.

'Who was that woman?' Jenny said. 'She looked at you as though she'd found you crawling around under a stone.'

'What woman?'

'The one who just came in and went out straight away.'

Bergerac looked round. The first person he saw was Tim Hobson, Susan's partner in the estate agency, crossing the room towards the counter. Hobson's eyes flicked over Bergerac and his companion. He shook his head sadly.

'Tallish,' Jenny went on with a casualness that deceived neither of them. 'Long, dark-red hair and a nice figure. Good clothes, too. All in all, rather attractive. If you like that sort of thing.'

'Oh, no.'

'So *that's* what she looks like.'

Bergerac sensed that Hobson was still watching them; you could almost see his gossip antennae twitching. He was probably on the verge of coming over to their table.

'Jenny, I've got to go,' Bergerac said. 'Can I give you a lift anywhere?'

'Yes, Jim,' she said meekly. 'You can give me a lift anywhere and anytime you like.'

CHAPTER
8

As Lady Wintersham poured the coffee, Charlie Hungerford surreptitiously admired the signed photograph of Edward VII on the mantelpiece.

He was in a much happier frame of mind – soothed partly by the excellence of the meal, but more by the consciousness that he was moving in a very select company indeed. Only a few governors were here – the inner circle that really mattered, together with Nigel Upperwood and Marcus Wintersham. Two of the governors had brought their wives; Virginia Upperwood had cried off at the last moment.

Wintersham was handing round the cups. He came over to Hungerford.

'What do *you* think, Charlie?' he asked in a low voice, carrying on the general discussion that had occupied most of dinner.

Hungerford shrugged, flattered to be asked. 'I know I'm a new boy here, as it were' – he paused for a second, hoping for a smile; but Marcus took the joke at face value – 'but to my mind there's no question about it. None at all. We've got to get the police in.'

Wintersham nodded. 'I agree. The Prankster's gone beyond a joke.'

'What does Lady Wintersham think?'

'She's coming round to the idea. But she's wondering if there's any way we can keep the publicity down.'

'It's worth a try, I'd say,' Hungerford said cautiously.

He had a shrewd idea of what was coming next. In his experience, human nature was the same the world over. The tactics that worked – to choose an example at random – in a back street in Leeds also worked in a millionaire's mansion on Jersey. You did things for other people, and they did things for you. And vice versa, of course. There were strings all around you: a wise man learned where they were and how to pull them.

'My aunt thought she might drop a word in the ear of Government House,' Wintersham said. 'And she's having tea with the Bailiff tomorrow; they're old friends.'

'That would help. But it's the States Police that really count, you know – they'd be doing the job. And then there's the media.'

Wintersham nodded.

'The Chief Officer's a friend of mine,' Hungerford said casually. 'He reports to my Committee, of course.'

'And the press . . . ?'

'I don't see much problem there – not in the short term, and not if we're all pushing in the same direction.' He glanced meaningfully at the sofa where Lady Wintersham was holding court.

'It occurred to me – just an idea – that Jim Bergerac might be quite a good man to have on the job.'

'Jim? Why?'

'He knows a lot of people already. He knows the school. His daughter's there, of course, so he's got a built-in reason to be discreet. We could even hint that his presence was something to do with the Yves case, if necessary.'

'Jim's Bureau,' Hungerford said. 'This would be a CID case.'

'In theory, perhaps. But one could argue that most of the pupils are only temporary residents and that the majority of the staff aren't exactly native to the island. I must say that Jim struck me as a very competent man.'

'He has his moments,' Hungerford said sourly, wondering if Wintersham meant 'tactful' rather than 'competent'; if he did, he was in for a shock. The real reason why the Wintershams wanted Bergerac was almost certainly because they believed that they could exercise, indirectly through Hungerford, some sort of influence over the investigating officer.

Keep it in the family. Hungerford's stomach churned at the memory of the letter and the tape, neither of which he had mentioned during the discussion about the Prankster's activities.

He was tempted to warn Marcus that Bergerac was about as biddable as the weather. One consideration held him back. At least Bergerac wouldn't want to harm Debby or Kim. So he could be relied upon to deal discreetly with the anonymous letter and the pornographic video.

'Good,' Marcus said. 'That's settled. By the way, my aunt was saying that you and Debby must come over for lunch sometime. Just the four of us, eh?'

Bergerac picked his way across the patch of wasteland towards the fire.

The fire had been cleverly sited. You could only see it if you approached from this direction. It was a cold night, made colder by the north-east wind, and Bergerac was wearing a heavy overcoat with deep pockets. The Indian summer ended when the sun went down.

As he drew nearer, a dark shape stirred against the flames. Newspaper rustled.

'Come any closer,' a hoarse, Irish voice whispered, 'and I'll brain you. I swear to God I will.'

'It's all right, Aloysius,' Bergerac said. He switched on the torch that he was carrying, angling the beam so that it illuminated his face. 'Just visiting.'

'Oh, God. Mr bloody Bergerac.'

There was a clatter as Aloysius dropped the iron bar on the ground. He squatted down, wrapping his khaki overcoat around him. Bergerac came nearer until he was within the radius of the fire's heat. He held out his hands to the blaze.

'Nice little place you've got here,' he said.

'Well, this *is* an honour,' Aloysius said. The voice was still Irish but it had lost its coarseness and become almost cultivated. The rough accent was a sort of protective colouring, adopted for life on the road. 'When they send the police to call on me at home, it's usually a brace of flatties, not a solitary busy. Your uniformed colleagues find safety in numbers.'

Bergerac dug into the pockets of his coat. He produced two cans of Carlsberg Special Brew and placed them upright on the ground, away from the heat of the fire but within easy reach of the Irishman.

'*Quidquid id est, timeo Danaos et dona ferentes*,' Aloysius said as he swept the cans towards him. 'The divine Virgil, Mr Bergerac. In these benighted days, few people can appreciate the beauties of the *Aeneid* in the original. I shall translate, freely yet accurately: "I fear the Constabulary when they bring me gifts, even cans of Special Brew." Where's the catch?'

'No catch. I just want to talk.'

Aloysius opened one of the cans and took a long swallow. 'They really should teach our policemen to be more precise.' He belched contentedly. 'You mean you want *me* to talk.'

Even on Jersey there were down-and-outs. The majority were not native but drifted over from the mainland to explore the island's dustbins and prey on the tourists; many of them, like Aloysius, were itinerant alcoholics. They lived for short periods in the cracks and corners of the social edifice, ignored and largely unseen by the Hungerfords and Wintershams who occupied the penthouse accommodation.

'I've got a problem,' Bergerac said. 'Maybe you can help.'

'I came here for a little peace and quiet.' Aloysius waved at the wasteland around him. 'Is it too much to ask? Anyway, how did you know where to find me?'

'I asked around your colleagues.'

The transients had their own customs, made their own laws and followed their own routines. Most were social animals that sought the society of their kind: a few, like Aloysius, were natural solitaries, savagely intent on their privacy. A good policeman came to know most of the regulars. Occasionally the fragile relationship between them could develop from a guarded tolerance to a form of friendship. Last autumn, Bergerac had saved Aloysius from the unwelcome attentions of a teenage gang.

'No police station,' Bergerac said. 'No court appearance. No publicity. Just two cans of Special Brew and maybe another two afterwards.'

'That is bribery,' Aloysius said with dignity. 'You confirm my worst fears. I have always maintained that our police force is corrupt. Even here, on this enchanted isle, this precious stone set in a silver sea.'

Unless he happened to be in jail, Aloysius always tried to be on Jersey for October. The summer, he had once explained to Bergerac, lingered longer here. He was clearly a man of education who from choice or necessity had adopted another mode of existence. Maybe he had been suddenly widowed or lost his job. Maybe he was looking for a sort of freedom or trying to drink himself to death. If he was in the mood, Aloysius would hold forth about anything under the sun – anything but his own past.

'You've been hanging around Mont Desir lately,' Bergerac said abruptly. He knew from experience that the more drink Aloysius consumed, the more flowery his language became and the more difficult it was to get any hard information out of him.

'True. An erotic name, I have always thought. I enjoy watching the tourists puffing and panting up that ramp to gawp at history. Usually for about five minutes, and then they've had enough; they find the past indigestible. Don't we all, Mr Bergerac? On Friday I derived a certain pleasure from reminding some of them that it was Friday the thirteenth. It was interesting to observe their reactions. I –'

'It's Thursday I'm interested in. Thursday morning.'

'Thursday. Should I remember Thursday? The day before Friday, of course. The days seem to blur into one another. Except Sundays, because the licensing hours are so difficult.'

'Maybe this will remind you.'

Bergerac pulled out the photograph that Pettit had developed. He passed it, together with the torch, to Aloysius. The Irishman stared at it for several seconds.

'The big event of the day,' he said. 'A coach had just arrived. Suddenly I had a wealth of specimens to observe. A cornucopia of raw material. A surfeit of human nature.'

'You mean you couldn't try and touch them all for the price of a drink?'

'You make it sound so unsubtle, Mr Bergerac. Believe me, there is an art to it.'

'I believe you. Do you remember the man you're talking to? The one with the camera case?'

Aloysius peered at the photograph. 'An ugly man, I recall, and proof against the blandishments of my art. I think it was he who called me a filthy little parasite. Or was that someone on Friday?'

'What I'd like to know,' Bergerac said, 'is whether it's the same man as this.'

He produced another photograph and passed it across.

Aloysius held it by the corner. 'This looks unpleasantly official,' he said with distaste. 'Am I right in thinking this is what you would no doubt call a mug-shot?'

Bergerac nodded.

Aloysius handed him both photographs.

'So nice to have had this little chat, Mr Bergerac. The weather has been quite clement for the time of year.'

'I'm not trying to put you in a witness box.' Bergerac grinned at the thought of Aloysius confronting a good defence counsel. 'All I want is a pointer in the right direction. Confirmation of a hunch, if you like. Are they the same man?'

He was putting the pressure on Aloysius – not in the words but in the tone he used. A policeman could make life very unpleasant for a transient, and both of them knew it.

'I'm sure I couldn't say. My memory isn't what it was, I'm afraid.'

'Try harder, Aloysius.'

The tramp stared into the fire, his arms wrapped round his knees. The flames emphasized the hollows in his face, making him seem gaunter than he was. A drop of moisture, tinted orange by the fire, hung from the tip of his nose. He sighed and swallowed some more lager.

'It's nothing personal, Mr Bergerac.' His voice had acquired a whine. 'I just don't want to get involved.'

That made a sort of sense. If you were on the road for any length of time you developed a deep-seated distrust of people in authority, especially when they wanted you to betray someone.

Bergerac dug into his pockets and produced two more cans of Carlsberg. 'This is off the record,' he said. 'Between ourselves.'

Aloysius eyed the cans.

'You wouldn't lie to me, would you?' Bergerac went on. 'Because sooner or later I'd find out.'

'Someone was killed at Mont Desir,' Aloysius said abruptly. 'That's why you want to know, isn't it?'

Bergerac nodded.

'In that case . . .' Aloysius scooped up the cans and thrust them into an inner pocket of his coat. 'My duty is clear. Yes indeed, they are the same man.'

'Thanks.'

Bergerac stood up, wondering whether he'd heard the truth or merely what Aloysius thought he would want to hear; and whether Aloysius refused to condone murder or was unable to resist the temptation of two cans of Carlsberg Special Brew. On his feet and away from the fire, he was exposed to the wind; he shivered as it cut through his clothes.

'It's a chilly night, Mr Bergerac,' Aloysius said, suddenly in the best of spirits. 'Can I offer you a nip to keep out the cold? A drop of the fluid that warms afore ye go?'

Virginia Upperwood was cold.

The wind rattled the window in its frame. She was sitting up in bed, with the duvet drawn up to her chin. Her feet rested on a hot-water bottle and the central heating was turned up. Still she was cold.

That was the trouble with these old houses. You never got properly warm. The rooms were big and draughty. She shuddered at the thought of the forthcoming winter. Why couldn't the governors provide the headmaster with a sensible modern house?

In the corner, the screen of a small television flickered with colour images; the sound was turned down to a murmur. She had a book on the bedside table and a pile of magazines on the bed. She couldn't concentrate on any of them. It wasn't the pills she had taken, though they weren't helping: it was the cold. There were goose pimples on her arms.

She glanced at the clock. It was only 11.30. Nigel was still at the Wintershams', doing what he did best – winning friends and influencing people. It was a pity he no longer used those talents on his wife. He had been infuriated by her refusal to come with him; her lips curled at the memory. Nigel wanted a consort. Denying him her company in public was a petty revenge, but it was one of the few ways she could hurt him.

It seemed to be growing colder. Somewhere in the distance she heard a muffled thud. It served as an unwelcome reminder that she was alone in the headmaster's wing. Come to think of it, she was probably alone in the whole house. No one else slept here.

The noise could have come from outside, she told herself firmly. Maybe she had imagined it. But she wasn't imagining the cold. Something had to be done about it. She gritted her teeth and got out of bed.

Once she was on her feet, the room seemed to sway. *Those damned pills.* But the cold and the change of position combined to have a bracing effect. She pulled on a heavy jersey over her pyjamas and found a quilted dressing-gown in the wardrobe.

Already she felt a little warmer. The small achievement whetted her appetite for more. Just this once, she wouldn't have another pill. She picked up the cooling hot-water bottle, opened the door and went downstairs to the kitchen.

The strip-lighting revealed her shortcomings: the pile of washing-up in the sink; the crumbs on the work surfaces; the dust on the supposedly clean mugs that hung from a shelf of the dresser; and the overflowing rubbish bin. Something was beginning to smell.

Virginia had a mad impulse to tidy up the kitchen. The impulse was as brief as it was uncharacteristic. She filled the kettle and rummaged in the cupboard until she found a saucepan that wasn't too grimy.

A fresh hot-water bottle, she thought, *and a cup of cocoa – with perhaps a tiny dash of brandy.*

While the milk was coming to the boil on the electric hob, she searched for the cocoa tin. It proved irritatingly elusive. Nigel must have put it somewhere. Bloody Nigel. The more she looked, the more her anger grew – and the more determined she was to have a cup of cocoa.

She was on her knees, investigating the back of the cupboard under the sink, when she heard the sound of a door closing softly, somewhere in the headmaster's wing of the house. Her first thought was that Nigel had returned and was creeping around in his usual slithery way.

But then, almost immediately, there was a muted bang and the lights went out.

Virginia swore. The noise of the kettle, which had been coming up to the boil, faded away. The electric ring, however, retained much of its heat, and the milk chose this moment to boil over.

She stood up and blundered across the kitchen, yelping as she caught her hip against the corner of the table. Probably the wiring in this mausoleum was only slightly younger than Noah's Ark. It was typical that the fuse should blow while Nigel was away. He could mend it himself when he got back from Lady Wintersham's. It would do him good to get his hands dirty for once. There was another refinement to the situation: she knew, from the early days of their marriage when they still talked to one another, that Nigel didn't like total darkness.

She reached the hob and gingerly lifted the saucepan away from the ring. It could have been worse: judging by the weight, there was enough left in the pan for a cup of warm milk; and the kettle would still be hot.

But some sort of light was needed. There were candles

and a torch in the cupboard under the stairs. With her hands outstretched before her, Virginia felt her way out of the kitchen and into the hall. The darkness made everything unfamiliar; it gave the world another shape. Your body became so vulnerable. *It must be horrible to be blind.*

The cupboard under the stairs was on the other side of the hall. As she was inching across the carpet, she realized suddenly that the darkness was not absolute. There was a dim light burning in Nigel's study.

Her first reaction was anger. He must have come back and found the torch when the power went; but he hadn't bothered to come upstairs and see if she was all right.

Guided by the light, she stormed across the hall and threw open the study door.

Her eyes could barely take in what they saw in the instant before the light was switched off. A small torch was shining at Nigel's desk, an antique he had inherited from his parents. For once, the top was clear of papers; they littered the carpet. The leather surface had been scored with a knife. Behind the desk, the drawers of the filing cabinet hung open.

The person holding the torch was in shadow; and in any case the open door prevented Virginia from getting a good view. Besides, there was no time to take it all in.

The torch snapped off, and everything was dark once more. There was a flurry of movement. Papers rustled underfoot. Virginia backed away and screamed.

Something struck her on the cheek, cutting her off in mid-scream. Virginia crumpled to the floor, automatically curling herself into a foetal position. The attacker kicked her several times in the back, and then bent down and punched her.

For a second, she felt warm breath against her ear: that, for some reason, was the worst thing about the whole episode.

Then there were running footsteps. The torch flashed. The front door opened and closed. Virginia was alone.

She lay there, trembling, for at least a minute. She was panting, as though she had run a mile. Blood trickled down her face. She was too shocked even to scream. Besides, there was no one to hear.

The darkness pressed down on her like a physical weight. This house was evil. Edward College was evil. She had to get away.

She concentrated her mind on the need to escape, clinging to the idea like a child clutches a security blanket. It was something positive. It was a solution. It stopped her from thinking about what had happened.

Moaning softly, she struggled to her feet. *Escape* – not just from this house but from the school. She stumbled along the hall to the alcove where the coats were kept.

Still shivering, she pulled on her fur coat over the dressing-gown; the added weight was oddly reassuring. Even better was the jingle of keys in the righthand pocket. *The car keys.*

Virginia Upperwood opened the front door and, leaving it ajar behind her, ran down the steps. The heels of her slippers slapped on the stone. It sounded as though someone was behind her. She ran faster, speeding across the gravel towards the row of staff garages.

It was only when she had started the engine that she realized what the next problem was. She knew what she was escaping from – but she had no idea where she would find safety.

For the first time that evening, Virginia began to cry.

At the Bureau des Etrangers, Detective Constable Ben Lomas was pretending that he was really at home.

He had his feet up on the desk and a computer magazine in his hands. His body twitched rhythmically in the chair;

he was listening to rock music on an all-night station. The congealing remains of an Indian takeaway were scattered across the desk. Lomas had made himself as comfortable as possible for the graveyard shift.

Bergerac pushed open the swing doors and swept into the office. A grin spread over Lomas's face as he took in Bergerac's windswept hair, shabby overcoat and heavy boots.

'You look like a tramp, Sarge.'

'That was the intention,' Bergerac said shortly. He switched off the radio. 'Any news?'

With maddening slowness, Lomas lifted his feet from the desk and tossed the magazine on the floor.

'There was a phone call,' he said vaguely. 'Someone at the Met.' He lifted one of the foil containers. 'I think I put it under the Special Basmati Rice. No, I tell a lie.' He lifted another. 'Mixed Vegetable Vhaji? No.' He lifted a third. 'Ah. Here we are. Chicken Birany. I might have known.'

Bergerac snatched the piece of paper from his hand. Lomas was technically on duty, so he was getting paid for wasting time; Bergerac wasn't. The paper was covered with a tangle of shorthand symbols. The message was the next best thing to illegible. Lomas's idiosyncratic shorthand was notorious among his fellow officers.

'You'd better decode this for me,' Bergerac said. 'And then you can type it out in full. Give you something to do.'

'But they'll be telexing the – '

'You heard me. Now, what did they say?'

Lomas scowled and took back the paper. 'Not much.' He frowned as he tried to decipher his own symbols. ' "Anthony Dodmarsh has been staying with friends in Hampshire since Tuesday. For friends, read associates. Judging by past form, he'll have a choice of cast-iron alibis up his sleeve for Thursday. Regards, Gordie." ' Lomas glanced up, his ill humour temporarily forgotten. 'Who *is* this character, Jim?'

'Dodmarsh? He's Mr Soho. Drugs, clubs, porn, prostitutes – you name it, he's got a stake. When they cleaned up Soho a bit, he just diversified to cover his losses. He's got bases in most of the big provincial cities on the mainland.'

'Thursday – can you connect him to Yves?'

Bergerac shook his head. 'Only to Mont Desir.' He pulled out the photograph that Pettit had developed. 'That's him, halfway up the ramp. But it wouldn't stand up in court, not by itself. No one on the coach remembers him, either; I've tried that.'

'What about the wino?'

'I've tried him, too. He says it's Dodmarsh, for what that's worth. But he's not going to stand up in a witness box and swear it. And even if he did, they'd rip his evidence to shreds.'

'I don't get it,' Lomas said. 'We've nothing to show that Yves was after Dodmarsh. And what was Dodmarsh doing at the castle?'

Bergerac shrugged. 'It'll give you something to think about in the wee small hours.'

The phone on Lomas's desk began to ring. Bergerac picked it up.

'Bureau.'

'That you, Jim?' It was Sergeant Corrance from reception. 'We've got one for you down here.'

'What is it?' Bergerac said wearily, reaching for a pad. Where Corrance was concerned, it paid to ask for details before accepting one of his referrals; the uniformed sergeant was renowned throughout the States Police for his habit of passing the buck.

'Woman from the mainland,' Corrance said smugly. 'Definitely Bureau. Looks like a right loony. She's got a fur coat over her pyjamas, and someone's bashed her face.'

'Can she hear you?'

'No – Jill's giving her a cup of tea. Anyway, she's round the bend. Says her life is in danger from a dangerous lunatic, and she demands police protection.'

Bergerac sighed. The Bureau had its fair share of paranoid housewives, just like every other police force. He would pass this one over to Lomas.

'Did you get a name and address out of her?'

'Upperwood,' Corrance said. 'Mrs Virginia Upperwood, from Edward College.'

The Prankster climbed the stairs with barely a sound.

Long experience had shown which treads squeaked, and how to cope with the darkness. Unwise to risk a light here.

The huge house was empty. By day it was the centre of Edward College; by night it was full of ghosts.

Upperwood wasn't back; his wife had run away; and the caretaker wasn't due to make his rounds until 12.30. The Prankster had waited to see what Mrs Upperwood did. Luckily, the stupid cow didn't go for help to one of the staff. (It had been so funny when she was rolling around on the floor.) Instead she drove down the drive and turned on to the main road. It was possible that she would return with the police. But the Prankster could rely on at least a few minutes' grace. Even if Mrs Upperwood came back sooner, it shouldn't be a problem: the Prankster knew all the exits; and besides, they'd have to find the main fuse boxes before they could do anything.

The Old Library was locked, but the Prankster had a key. The first thing to do was to draw the heavy curtains. Then it would be safe to risk the torch. The beam bounced off the highly polished table, around which the governors sat.

The Prankster opened the knife and walked down the table, scraping the tip of the blade through the varnish and into the wood beneath. The light was reflected in the glass-fronted bookcases. It was tempting to attack those neat, leather-bound volumes; but there wasn't time.

First things first. Hit them where it hurts.

The Prankster had reached the end of the room. There, behind the high-backed chair where Lady Wintersham sat, was Sargent's portrait of the Jersey Rose. The torch beam slid up to the face.

The fat old bitch is laughing at me . . .

The Prankster reversed the knife and smashed the haft against it. The sound of breaking glass was shockingly loud in the silent house. The Prankster used the blade to scrape away more glass.

At last the Jersey Rose was quite defenceless. The Prankster began work.

CHAPTER
9

On the morning of Sunday the 15 October, there was a public display organized by the Jersey Model Aero Club at St Ouen's Bay. It was a perfect day for model aircraft – bright and windless. One of the club's most enthusiastic members was not there. His brand-new Lancaster bomber remained unseen and unflown in the boot of his car. Instead, he was in an office on the top floor of Police Headquarters in Rouge Bouillon.

'Sorry to drag you in, Barney,' the Superintendent said; his West Country burr was more pronounced than usual – a sure sign that he was annoyed. It was clear by his clothes that he hadn't expected to come into the office, either. 'Sit down and have some coffee.'

'Trouble?'

'You could say that.' He poured a cup for Crozier before continuing. 'Our lords and masters are breathing down our necks. Not to put too fine a point on it, they're telling us how to do our jobs.'

It was then that Crozier realized belatedly that the Superintendent wasn't just annoyed at the loss of his Sunday morning: for some unknown reason, he was quietly furious.

'The Committee are leaning on us?' Crozier glanced across the desk that separated them. 'It's not something to do with that crazy plan to amalgamate the Bureau with CID?'

'Nothing like that. And it's not just the Committee we

have to worry about. Though there might be ramifications: if you want to keep your autonomy, I'd advise you to play along.'

'With what?'

'With what Charlie Hungerford wants. *And* Lady Wintersham. *And* all their friends, who apparently include anyone on this island with the slightest bit of political or financial clout.' The Superintendent grimaced; anger had made him unusually loquacious. 'It's not just us they're ganging up on. I gather that the media have been told to toe the line, too.'

'So what do they want?' Crozier asked.

'They've got a mucky little scandal at Edward College. Someone they call "The Prankster" is on the loose. Anonymous letters, arson, attacks on property – and last night the headmaster's wife was mugged.'

Crozier made a break for the one escape route in sight: 'Edward College is a school – it's not really within the Bureau's jurisdiction. It's a CID job, surely?'

The distinction meant nothing to the Superintendent, who was responsible for both departments; but it could mean a great deal to Crozier.

The older man shook his head. 'It's primarily a boarding-school, and it's in the private sector, so the jurisdiction's in dispute. It's a purely technical question, in any case. As far as we're concerned, the important thing is that the Powers-That-Be want the Bureau.' The ghost of a smile touched his mouth. 'If you think about it, Barney, that's quite a compliment. To you and the Bureau.'

'It's the sort of compliment we can do without.' Crozier was privately rather pleased with it, nevertheless. 'Do we know how long all this has been going on?'

'Weeks.' The Superintendent shrugged his heavy shoulders. 'More or less since the beginning of term. And now they decide to tell us. *Now* they want an investigation – a discreet, under-the-carpet job, if it's humanly possible, or even if it isn't.'

'We can't do that.'

'So I told the Chief. But he said we could. The official reason is that the pupils' parents bring in a small fortune: they invest here, as well as farm their brats out. So we have to keep them sweet. Unofficially we're supposed to ignore the facts that Lady Wintersham's the chairman of the governors and takes a maternal interest in the school; that Hungerford's on the board; and that both of them have got brats of their own there.'

'Can't we fight it?'

'In theory. And we'd probably win.' The Superintendent hesitated for a second. He looked like a man that has just swallowed the worm in the apple. 'But only at the cost of antagonizing almost everyone that's anyone on this island.'

Crozier sipped his coffee to give him time to think. He liked to think of himself as a realist; and as such he had no objection in principle to doing what the Superintendent wanted, as long as he personally was covered.

The Superintendent had carefully avoided giving him an order: this was a request, and therefore Crozier would be within his rights to turn it down. In many ways he would have liked to do so, because this sort of case was notoriously difficult to solve; the criminal's motives weren't in any way rational, nor were his methods.

On the other hand, there were other implications, as the Superintendent had hinted. If Crozier wanted to keep the Bureau independent and under his control, he really had no option but to cooperate. Moreover — to take the long term view, as Crozier usually did where his career was concerned — the Superintendent wouldn't last for ever: he was due to retire in just over four years' time; Crozier knew the exact month. Someone would have to replace him — probably one of the existing Chief Inspectors in the States

Police. Why not Barney Crozier? It would pay to have friends in high places.

But there was no point in sounding too enthusiastic.

'I suppose we have no real choice, sir,' Crozier said. 'Can we get anything in writing?'

The Superintendent nodded. 'Don't worry. I'll see that we're covered if the story does leak out.'

'I'd better take the case myself,' Crozier said.

'I've had a request on that subject,' the Superintendent said with a trace of embarrassment. 'As a matter of fact – '

He was interrupted by the phone. With a snort of exasperation he seized the handset.

'I thought I said no calls.'

Crozier couldn't hear what was being said on the other end.

'All right,' the Superintendent said wearily. 'Put him through.' He switched on the desk-top speaker and covered the mouthpiece with his hand. 'It's the headmaster at Edward College.' He uncovered the mouthpiece. 'Mr Upperwood? What can I do for you?'

'We've just discovered another outrage, Superintendent – in the Old Library.' Upperwood's voice quivered with shock. 'I really don't know how we can tell Lady Wintersham.'

'What exactly's happened, sir?'

'The Prankster must have got in during the night. The table's scratched – not that that matters. But he's *destroyed* the Jersey Rose.'

The Superintendent raised his eyebrows at Crozier. 'I beg your pardon, sir?'

'The Sargent portrait! It's ruined – slashed with a knife. Quite apart from the painting's intrinsic value, the aesthetic damage is *incalculable*.'

'Dear me,' the Superintendent said. 'You'd better keep the room locked, sir. We'll send someone round as soon as we can.' He said goodbye and put down the phone with a sigh. 'He's more worried about the painting than he was about the attack on his wife. As I was saying: we've been requested to put Sergeant Bergerac on the case.'

'But he's investigating the Yves murder.'

'You'll have to hand it over to someone else.'

Crozier grinned. 'He's not going to like it. Do they know what they're letting themselves in for?'

The Superintendent's mouth gave an answering twitch. 'I don't think they do. But that's their problem. By the way, is there any progress on that front?'

'Not much.' Crozier had glanced at the updated file on the case before coming upstairs; he had assumed that the Yves murder was why the Superintendent had summoned him on a Sunday morning. 'Jim says the only person with a known motive for killing Yves is Lady Wintersham.'

'*What?*'

'I think he's almost serious. Apparently, Yves was trying to prove that the Jersey Rose was a fraud – that she'd lied about being a King's mistress. And Jim says he may well have been right. So Lady Wintersham wouldn't have any royal blood.'

'For God's sake! That's not a motive!'

'It's the best he's managed to come up with. It's true the woman *does* worship her ancestors, and the royal connection gives the school a bit of snob appeal. But there's another point: we've evidence to suggest that Anthony Dodmarsh was at Mont Desir on the morning Yves was killed.'

'Now that is interesting. "Suggest"?'

'Just that, sir. Not a hope of proving it at present. We've checked with the Met.'

'You saw that memo from the Chief? The one about the importing of hard porn?'

Crozier nodded. 'It's tempting.'

'It's more than that: it makes your mouth water. The

Met. would give us the keys of the kingdom if we could tie in Dodmarsh with that racket. Keep at it.'

'I'd better get in touch with Jim,' Crozier said. 'He's meant to be off-duty.'

'He's not at that cottage of his – I've tried.'

'I'll phone around.'

'All right. And thanks, Barney.'

Crozier left the room. On the whole, he was pleased with the way the interview had gone. He hadn't made it easy for the Superintendent; but he hadn't made it difficult, either. It was always wise to keep them guessing for as long as you could – the Superintendent hadn't been able to predict the reaction to his request. All in all, Crozier was inclined to think that he had just climbed another invisible rung on the ladder that would lead eventually to a chief constable's office and possibly – why think small? – even to a knighthood.

But, as he clattered down the stairs, an unwelcome thought occurred to him: if the Superintendent had already tried to get in touch with Bergerac, then the old man must have taken his, Crozier's, cooperation for granted.

Charlie Hungerford opened the front door and peered furtively at his visitor.

'Why all the mystery?' Bergerac said. 'You expecting the bailiffs?'

'It's not funny, Jim. I can do without your cheap cracks.' Hungerford realized that he had made a tactical error and belatedly tried to make up for it. 'Mark you, I'm very grateful you've come, and I shan't forget it.'

'I still don't understand why you didn't drive over to my house if it was so urgent.'

'You will.' Hungerford led Bergerac to the library. 'Debby's out,' he said over his shoulder. 'She and Marcus are playing squash, or something.' He glanced around the big room as though searching for an excuse to postpone whatever he had to say. 'Oh – I nearly forgot. Barney Crozier wants you to phone him at the Bureau.'

'Why?'

'He didn't say.'

Bergerac looked sharply at his ex-father-in-law: he knew when Charlie was being shifty; he also knew there was no point in trying to press him. He dialled Rouge Bouillon and was put through to the Bureau.

Crozier gave him a swift briefing about the Prankster at Edward College, and told him to get over there as soon as he had finished with Hungerford.

'What about the . . . other business?' Bergerac said. He would have said a lot more if Hungerford had not been in the room.

'I'll handle the Yves case for the moment.'

'But Barney – '

'No "buts", Sergeant. Not now. This comes from the top. There are wheels within wheels.'

'There always are.' Bergerac looked venomously at Hungerford. 'Is this anything to do with a certain Committee?'

'If you must know, yes.' Crozier's voice softened in an attempt to be diplomatic. 'Look, Jim, I'll fill you in properly when you get back from Edward College. Just do it, will you?'

Bergerac replaced the handset without replying.

'You've been pulling strings again,' he said to Hungerford. 'Just to oblige Lady Wintersham?'

'Well, never mind that now, Jim. I've got some evidence for you.'

'You've got . . . Oh, I get it. The poison-pen's put you on his list of correspondents.'

Hungerford flushed. 'It's not funny. Believe me, it's damned unsettling to feel there's someone out there who hates you so much.' He unlocked the safe. 'It makes you realize you can trust no one.'

'When did you get it?'

'Eh? Oh, yesterday morning.'

'And you waited till today to tell the police.'

'It's embarrassing. Besides . . .'

'You wanted to calculate all the angles first?'

'There's no need to sound so bloody censorious,' Hungerford snapped. 'Naturally I wanted to find out if other people had had them. It makes it – ah – less personal, if you know what I mean.'

'Can't say I do, Charlie.'

'Well, you never were exactly sensitive about other people's feelings.' Hungerford pulled himself up with an effort. 'Sorry. I'm a bit on edge. The point is, I had dinner with Lady Wintersham last night – ' despite the circumstances, a faint note of pride crept into his voice ' – just me and one or two other governors and Nigel Upperwood. Oh, and Marcus was there, too. Bit of a Council of War, really – we had to decide how we were going to handle this Prankster business. And – just as I suspected – other people, all connected with the school, had had anonymous letters.'

'I could have told you that myself,' Bergerac said, remembering Ted Poolstock's letter.

Hungerford took an envelope from the top shelf of the safe and handed it gingerly to Bergerac.

'No one else has handled it,' he said, 'apart from me.'

Bergerac read the letter, folded it up and put it in his pocket.

Hungerford was watching him anxiously. 'Filthy business, isn't it?'

Bergerac nodded.

'There won't be any publicity, will there?'

'We won't tell if you don't.'

Hungerford flushed again. 'That sort of rubbish is so dangerous. Mud sticks in a place this size, however ridiculous it is. Think what it could do to Debby.'

'Charlie,' Bergerac said. 'Don't worry, OK? We're paid to keep our mouths shut. Anyway, no one would believe an allegation like this.'

'Some people,' Hungerford said darkly, 'will believe *anything*.'

'Don't think about it.' Bergerac moved towards the door. 'I'll drop this off at the lab when I get back to headquarters.'

'Don't go yet – there's something else.' Hungerford swallowed. 'Something worse.'

Bergerac frowned. 'Another letter?'

'No – it's this.' Hungerford held up the video tape he had taken from the safe. 'Jim – this may not be police business at all. It's family.' The flush had receded, leaving his face mottled. Suddenly he looked like an old man. 'I'm worried about Kim.'

His hands shook as he fed the tape into the VCR. Bergerac guessed that the VCR was Hungerford's reason for wanting him to come here; he didn't have one at the cottage. Then he stopped watching Hungerford and started watching the TV screen.

A minute was enough. It was more than enough. Hungerford sat down heavily in an armchair. Bergerac switched off the machine and ejected the tape. He examined the plastic casing carefully.

'I've already done that,' Hungerford said. 'It's as plain as the nose on your face. Someone peeled off the labels from my *High Society* and put them on *that*. I just put the tape on, yesterday evening, and there it was.' He licked his lips. 'That chain saw . . . I don't mind telling you, I felt sick. Physically ill.'

'I don't blame you. It's a snuff movie.'

'A what?'

'A pornographic movie,' Bergerac said softly, 'where somebody is killed at the climax. Usually a woman or even a girl. And they don't just die on the film. It's for real.'

'But surely, the police . . . ?'

'It's not easy to stop. All you need's a video camera and somewhere private. And a victim, of course. That's the easy part: you can rent anonymous flesh in any city. I think this one's West German, judging by the cartons at the back of the garage.'

Hungerford's voice rose with outrage. 'But what sort of animals would want to watch it?'

'There's plenty. It's big business, Charlie. Low overheads. High turnover. Surprisingly little risk. The punters are prepared to pay the earth for the privilege of watching someone die.'

For a few seconds the room was silent. Then Bergerac, who was moving restlessly from the windows to the door and back again, asked the question that Hungerford didn't want to answer.

'So where does Kim come into this?'

Hungerford stirred in his chair. 'They've got some sort of film club at Edward College. I lent her *High Society*. She sent it back via Debby on Friday night.'

'Does Debby know?'

'About the tape? Yes, I told her this morning.'

This time the silence was longer. Both men were thinking the same thing.

'Maybe . . .' Hungerford said. 'Maybe I was wrong about wanting her at Edward College. The move must have upset her more than we realized. Or maybe it's a delayed reaction to your divorce. I don't know. I thought I *knew* her.' He gathered momentum as he talked; talking was safer than thinking. 'Last night, Upperwood said she was involved in at least two of the other incidents . . . Something about throwing soup over a boy in the dining hall on Saturday. I had no idea she had a *violent* streak, did you? Makes you realize – we're all strangers. Of course, it might just be a temporary phase. It probably is, I'd say. A lot of adolescents are disturbed, in one way or another. Take poltergeists, for example, or – or – tantrums. Debby was *unbelievable* when she was sixteen. I'm sure we can manage something – least said, soonest mended, that's my motto. A change of scene would – '

'Shut up, Charlie!' Bergerac shouted.

Hungerford blinked. 'I was only trying – '

'I know. Trying to help. But you're prejudging this. You can't be sure that Kim's the Prankster.'

'No. Not sure. Not quite.'

CHAPTER
10

The Mercedes crept up the drive of Heartland House, forked left where the drive divided, passed through a round-headed archway and rolled to a halt on the cobbles of what had once been the stableyard.

It was another brilliantly sunny day, and Debby had the soft-top down. Her squash kit was on the back seat. Before she had met Marcus, she had thought that squash was one of those violent competitive activities that were best avoided by sensible people. Now she was not so sure. Marcus made her want to stop being sensible.

A door closed and she looked up. A flight of stone steps led up to the first floor of the coach-house, where the main entrance was. Marcus waved down at her. He was carrying his kit, and over his shoulder was the black-leather case that held his camera equipment. She waved back, feeling suddenly breathless, as though she were sixteen and he were the boy next door.

He ran down the steps, leant into the car and kissed her. 'Let's get away,' he said. 'Will you drive?'

'OK. What's the hurry?'

'There's a flap on at Edward College. Hasn't your father mentioned it?'

She shook her head. 'I've hardly seen him this morning.'

She shut away the memory of what her father had said about the video tape, just before she left. It wasn't the tape itself: it was the implications. At present she didn't want to talk about it to anyone. Even Marcus.

117

He walked round the car, slung his belongings into the back and got into the passenger seat. 'Someone's been playing nasty practical jokes, and we're calling the police in. If we hang around much longer, my aunt's going to summon me over there.'

'What sort of jokes?'

'Well, last night Virginia Upperwood was attacked, and the Sargent portrait of the Jersey Rose was vandalized. It's getting serious.'

Debby shivered. 'Is she all right? Mrs Upperwood, I mean.'

'Just shocked, really. Understandably enough. She's staying in a hotel. Apparently she's sworn never to go near Edward College again.'

'I don't blame her. Any idea who's behind it?'

Marcus shrugged. 'The field's wide open.'

Debby started the engine and drove slowly out of the yard. It was as well that she was driving slowly because, as she rounded the blind corner after the archway, she had to brake sharply.

'Oh no,' Marcus murmured. 'So much for the fast getaway.'

Theodore Poolstock was on his hands and knees in the middle of the drive, with a bewildered expression on his face. His briefcase had disgorged its contents on to the gravel. He was surrounded by a sea of papers.

He looked up at the car. 'I tripped,' he said. 'Those stones on the edge of the drive are really most dangerous.'

The borders of the drive were defined by rows of granite blocks, each a yard apart from its neighbours.

Marcus was already out of the car. 'Nothing broken?'

'I don't think so. I suppose I must count myself fortunate. At my age, even the slightest tumble can have terrible consequences. A friend of mine broke his hip only the other day. And do you know what he was doing? Merely getting out of bed!'

He allowed Marcus to help him up. He brushed ineffectually at his clothes, clicking his tongue against the roof of his mouth. Meanwhile Debby got out of the car and began to pick up the papers.

'Thank you, Mrs . . . er,' Poolstock said. 'Do try to keep them in order, won't you?' He straightened his tie. 'I've just sorted them out,' he told Marcus with a sigh. 'No easy task, I assure you, with something of this magnitude.'

Marcus helped Debby restore the papers to the case.

'A defective catch,' Poolstock said bitterly. 'I shall complain to the manufacturers. It sprang open when it hit the gravel. It's just not good enough. My time is too valuable to waste.'

'Can we give you a lift?' Marcus asked.

'That would be most kind. I only came here to pick up some papers – I plan to work in the Old Library today. Yes, even on Sunday,' he continued, in answer to a question that no one had asked, 'the work must go on.'

'I'm not sure they'll let you work there today. Have you heard about the Jersey Rose?'

Poolstock hadn't. It took a minute to tell him about the Prankster's latest exploit, and a further five minutes for him to digest the news and express his outrage.

'It's so inconsiderate,' he said. 'I suppose I shall have to work in the Wintersham Library instead.'

Marcus got into the back of the car. Poolstock settled himself beside Debby and struggled with the catch of the safety-belt.

'You're off to play squash?' Poolstock said as the car pulled away. 'I fear my sporting days are long since over.'

'Mine never really began,' Debby said. 'But Marcus is very tactful on court: he doesn't make me feel too much of a fraud.'

Poolstock swivelled his head to look at Marcus; talking with women made him feel uncomfortable. 'Is that a camera in there?' he asked, nodding at the black-leather case. 'I thought you had some sort of metal container for it. Didn't I see you with it the other day?'

'Probably. I've got two. We're going on to St Ouen before lunch, to see if we can get some shots of the Model Aero Club's display.'

'Nasty little things,' Poolstock said. 'They buzz like hornets. You're quite a dab hand with a camera, aren't you?'

Marcus shrugged. 'I take a lot of pictures, but I wouldn't say I ranked as an expert.'

The car turned right out of the drive. Debby glanced in the rear mirror, and saw Mont Desir framed there like a stone monster about to spring into the sea.

'I wonder if you could help me,' Poolstock went on. 'Lady Wintersham is very keen to have a section of black-and-white plates in the biography. Old family photographs – modern pictures of Edward College – that sort of thing. I'd value your advice. Perhaps you could even take some – ah – snapshots for the book.'

Marcus's eyes met Debby's in the rear-view mirror. She suppressed a smile. Marcus had been living in fear that, one way or another, he would be asked to help with Poolstock's magnum opus.

'Of course,' he said. 'It'd be a pleasure.'

'Good,' Poolstock said briskly; he had obviously taken Marcus's agreement for granted. 'We must discuss the matter – perhaps this week? I could fit you in on Tuesday afternoon.'

Debby slowed for the turn into Edward College.

'I'm afraid I have a meeting then,' Marcus said quickly. 'We'll take you over to the Wintersham Library, shall we? Save you the walk.'

Again, his eyes met Debby's. She knew precisely what was in his mind. If they went on to the main house, there was a far greater chance that someone would hijack him to help with the Prankster investigation.

She pulled up outside the modern block that housed the new library and the sixth-form centre. It was curiously unsettling to think that for most of the year this place was Kim's home. She remarked to Poolstock that the school seemed unusually empty.

'They're all in chapel,' the old man said. 'If you can call it that, nowadays.'

'Nigel Upperwood's instituted a new, multi-denominational service for Sunday mornings,' Marcus explained.

Poolstock snorted. 'In my time, the Church of England was quite good enough for us.'

He got out of the car. Marcus handed him his briefcase and then scrambled over the seats into the front.

'Thank you so much, Mrs . . . er,' Poolstock began. 'It was most – '

'Drive on,' Marcus hissed.

Debby glanced at the wing mirror. Lady Wintersham had just emerged from the main house and was walking briskly across the grass towards them. She waved at them to stop.

The Mercedes shot away, cutting short Mr Poolstock's elaborate vote of thanks in mid-paragraph.

'That was a close shave.' Marcus grinned at Debby, and she was suddenly happier than she had been for years. 'Now we can really enjoy ourselves.'

The three of them met at midday in the headmaster's study.

Upperwood, an imposing figure in the academic gown and hood he wore for chapel, stood by the empty fireplace;

Lady Wintersham occupied the armchair nearby; and Bergerac preferred to stand near the door.

'Have your men finished in the Old Library yet?' Lady Wintersham demanded. 'Ted Poolstock wants to use it.'

'Give us until lunchtime,' Bergerac said.

'Have they found anything?'

Bergerac shook his head. 'Whoever it was had a key, and wore rubber gloves.' He looked at Upperwood. 'I want to talk to some of your sixth formers.'

'Very well. You suspect one of them?'

Bergerac tapped James Doncaster's schedule of the Prankster's exploits; Upperwood had passed it on to him. 'I think we can narrow it down to the sixth form, the teaching staff or the domestic staff. The lower forms are too heavily supervised to get away with it.'

'There's another possibility,' Lady Wintersham interrupted. 'An outsider. Someone with a grudge against the school or what it stands for.'

'We have considered that. But I don't think it's likely. Your security's too good. I've checked it myself.'

Lady Wintersham frowned, unwilling to give up her theory. 'I must say,' she went on, 'I'm disappointed that you've made so little progress.'

'We've only been here for an hour or so,' Bergerac snapped. 'Besides, you should have called us in weeks ago.'

'Perhaps you're right,' she conceded unexpectedly. 'What do you intend to do?'

'Check out as many of these incidents as we can. Comb through your records – both staff and students – and see if we can come up with anyone with a history of mental illness. I think we can assume that whoever's behind this is not entirely sane.'

Upperwood glanced at Lady Wintersham. 'We can't just throw open our records to all and sundry, Sergeant. They're confidential.'

Bergerac had intercepted that glance. He was willing to bet that there was something they weren't telling him. Something to do with Virginia Upperwood? Could she have faked the attack on herself? It would be interesting to see if the incidents stopped while she was away from Edward College.

'This is a police investigation, sir,' he said, willing himself to be patient. 'And we're confidential, too. Next, we can organize patrols of the school, perhaps with the help of some of the teaching staff. Finally, I'd like to search the whole place.'

'Impossible,' said Lady Wintersham. 'It would attract just the sort of publicity we're trying to avoid. Besides, it would be an intolerable invasion of privacy.'

'My sentiments exactly,' Upperwood said.

Bergerac kept hold of his temper. 'There's one more thing. I may have to resign from the case.'

'You can't do that, Sergeant.' Lady Wintersham's eyebrows shot up. 'You've hardly begun.' A conciliatory note crept into her voice. 'I dare say that we may be able to find a way to meet your – '

'It's not that. It's a possible conflict of interests. As you know, my daughter's at the school.'

Kim Bergerac was sitting alone in the dining hall, trying to eat her lunch. She wasn't hungry. She was only eating because she was damned if she would give up and run away to the safety of her own room.

The dining hall was crowded – people tended to eat early on Sundays to make the afternoon as long as possible – but there was no one sitting beside her or opposite her. In the last twenty-four hours, the word had gone round. They were leaving her in isolation.

'Honk, honk,' Chris Gunter said behind her, as he

walked along the table towards Rose Wintersham. 'The piglet's at the trough.'

Rose grinned at him. Soon they were sitting together, deep in conversation. Every now and then, one of them glanced surreptitiously at Kim.

A tray slid on to the table beside her. Kim looked up. It was Akbar Farzanah.

'Are you sure you want to eat with me?' she said. 'I'm in quarantine, or didn't you know?'

He began to butter his roll. 'Do you want to go into St Helier this afternoon?'

'Didn't you hear what I said? You'd better keep away: I'm dangerous to know. They all think I'm the Prankster.'

'Well, I don't.' Akbar smiled at her. 'Are you going to eat that stuff, or just push it round the plate?'

Kim bit her lip. 'It's so *bloody* unfair. They're saying that I vandalized my room to throw them off the scent. It was Chris Gunter who started all this. He and Rose Wintersham.'

'They can't help being mentally retarded. The best thing to do is carry on as normal. So that's what we'll do. OK?'

'OK.' She smiled at him, grateful that he was not only prepared to believe her but ready to parade his belief in front of Edward College. She tried another mouthful of salad and almost managed to enjoy eating it.

Mr Doncaster had come into the dining hall. He looked around and came over to Rose and Chris. Kim stiffened, wondering if Upperwood had summoned them again. After he had finished with them Doncaster came over to Kim and Akbar.

'The police would like to see you both this afternoon,' he said. 'Nothing to worry about. They're using the secretary's office.'

The police. Kim could imagine what Rose and Chris would tell them.

'What time?' Akbar asked.

'Three o'clock for you, and ten past for Kim. It's just routine – they've already grilled me.'

'That blows St Helier,' Kim said, as lightly as she could.

'*You*'ll be all right,' Doncaster said to her. 'One of them's your dad.'

Kim nodded, bowing her head so Doncaster couldn't see her face. The master walked away.

Akbar patted her shoulder. At that moment, Rose Wintersham passed behind them on her way to the door.

'Piglet,' she murmured, with a sniff.

Bergerac pushed open the door. What he was doing was unorthodox; it might even earn him an official reprimand if Crozier got to hear of it. But nothing was orthodox about this investigation.

The first thing that struck him about Kim's room was its tidiness. She was never like this at home. Maybe Edward College had something to be said for it after all. Then he remembered that the room had been hit by the Prankster yesterday afternoon. Kim must have been forced to tidy it up.

As he had been trained, he searched in a clockwise direction from the door. But police-college training had never covered the subject of how you searched your own daughter's room. As a parent he was prying; as a policeman he was doing his job. And somehow he felt out of line in both roles.

He left the door ajar and worked quickly. He ought to have brought in Goddard or someone as a witness; that was the bare minimum that the rule-book demanded. Most people were having lunch; with luck he wouldn't get caught in the act.

None of her shoes was stained with white gloss paint; none of her clothes smelled of petrol. If she owned a sharp knife and a pair of rubber gloves, they weren't kept here. She had a torch, but the battery had long since gone flat and leaked over the terminals at either end. Her stationery – which, together with the leather case that held it, was a present from her doting grandfather – was Three Candlesticks, at the other end of the scale from the cheap paper and envelopes that the Prankster used for his correspondence. He found neither scissors nor glue in the desk.

In the waste-paper basket, however, there was a torn-up photograph. Bergerac reassembled the fragments: he recognized Kim's current boyfriend from the mainland. The fact that his picture had been consigned, unmended, to the waste-paper basket suggested that the boy now belonged to history. Bergerac tossed the pieces away. As a father, he couldn't help wondering who the new boyfriend was.

He moved to the bed, tugging it a few inches away from the wall. Paper rustled. A ball of newspaper lay on the carpet beneath; it must have been wedged between the bedframe and the wall. There was dust on the carpet – it looked as if the bed had not been moved out for some time. Bergerac picked up the newspaper and smoothed it out.

It was a double-page from the *Post*, a little over a fortnight old. Someone had snipped dozens of words and letters from it, so the paper was studded with irregularly spaced and oddly sized windows.

Bergerac sat down heavily on the bed. He was looking at the raw material for the Prankster's letters.

CHAPTER
11

Rose Wintersham paused when she reached the door. She looked with interest at both Bergerac and Goddard, as if assessing their worth on some private scale of values. '*So sorry I can't help*,' she said. 'You will let me know if there's *anything* I can do, won't you?'

She batted her eyelashes at them, sniffed and left the room.

After the door had closed, Goddard said softly: 'I wouldn't care to get too close to that one. If you kissed her, she'd give you more than her cold.'

'Maybe,' Bergerac said. 'But not an obvious candidate for the Prankster.'

Goddard nodded. 'Just room for one thought in her head – if that's the part of her anatomy she thinks with. I suppose she takes after Granny.'

'The Jersey Rose? That's Great-Granny.'

'Same difference. Shall I get the next one in?'

Bergerac grunted. He hoped to God that he was acting normally. Barry Goddard knew him too well for comfort. Bergerac was concealing evidence, or at least postponing its discovery, and it wasn't easy. He needed time to think.

Chris Gunter lounged into the room. He refused the offer of a chair. The interview that followed was short but not exactly sweet. Bergerac took down the details about yesterday's arson attack on the boy's room. Gunter went out of his way to be offensive. He also found ways to drop Kim's name into his replies.

'What's bugging you?' Bergerac said at last.

'This whole set-up,' Gunter said. 'It stinks.'

'How come?'

'Well, it's not what you'd call an unbiased investigation. You're Kim's dad, aren't you?' His mouth twisted in a sneer. 'So much for the great traditions of impartial British justice.'

'Out,' Bergerac said softly.

'What?'

'I said, get out.'

Gunter shrugged. 'It'll be my pleasure.'

The door slammed behind him.

Goddard looked at the floor.

'He's right,' Bergerac said. 'It's a conflict of interests.'

'You don't think that Kim – ?'

'Gunter does. He made that clear enough, if only by what he didn't say.'

'Take no notice of him.' Goddard jerked his thumb at the door. 'He's been watching too many James Dean films.'

'OK, so he's an aggressive adolescent with a big mouth: but that doesn't mean he's wrong. Besides, it's not just the fact that Kim's involved. I don't like the idea that Charlie Hungerford and Lady Wintersham are pulling the strings.'

'It's just a job, Jim.' Goddard, like Crozier, fancied himself as a realist; he intended to go far in the States Police and probably would. 'Take it easy.'

Bergerac thought of the mutilated sheet of newsprint that was tucked in his inside pocket. This wasn't just a job. It was a nightmare. The only answer was to have it out with Barney Crozier – tell him that he was resigning from the case. And why. But how would that affect Kim? By themselves, the innuendoes, the video tape and the newspaper proved nothing, but they were enough to turn the harsh glare of suspicion on her.

The next interview was easier. Akbar Farzanah, whom

Bergerac had met briefly on Friday evening, seemed to have left the awkwardness of adolescence behind. He answered Bergerac's questions about the incident in the Wintersham Library with a grave courtesy that belonged to a far older person.

On Friday night, he had been unable to sleep. He had read for a while and then switched out the light and stared out of the window. His room overlooked the entrance to the Wintersham Library. A flash of light caught his attention. It might have been someone shining a torch on the lock of the door. Next he saw a shadow moving along the line of the building. It disappeared round the corner.

'Man or woman?' Bergerac asked.

'I don't know. It was just a shadow. Dark clothes, maybe – lighter ones would have stood out. I think the face must have been covered, or at least blackened.'

'How about the height?'

'Sorry – I was looking down, you see, so it was impossible to judge how tall he was. Or she.'

'And you woke Mr Doncaster right away?'

Akbar nodded. 'He's got rooms in the sixth-form centre.'

Bergerac continued with the questions, but he got nothing useful out of him. Finally, he asked Goddard if there was anything he wanted to ask.

'There's just one thing.' He mouthed a single word at Bergerac: '*McCann.*'

Bergerac nodded. The Bureau owed the CID's drug squad a favour.

'Do you know of a pub called the Golden Ball?' Goddard said.

'It's the nearest pub to the school,' Akbar said. 'Why?'

'Ever been there?'

'Once or twice.' He saw the next question in Goddard's face, and answered it before it was put into words: 'Not by myself – I'm only seventeen. People from the Upper Sixth go there sometimes.'

'You're allowed to go to pubs?' Goddard said incredulously.

'Since Mr Upperwood came, yes. You're supposed to ask permission, of course, and you have to go in a party with a leader, usually a teacher, who's responsible for the rest of you.' He grinned, which made him look much younger. 'That's the theory, anyway. According to Upperwood, if something's forbidden, it becomes fatally attractive.'

'OK,' Bergerac said. 'Well, thanks for coming in.'

Akbar stood up. He hesitated by the door.

Bergerac looked up. 'Is there something else?'

'There are a lot of rumours going round the school,' Akbar said. 'I . . . I shouldn't pay too much attention to them.'

Bergerac stared at him for a second. 'We won't.'

When they were alone, Goddard said, 'What did he mean by that?'

'I think he meant Kim. My guess is that she's having a rough time and he wants to stop it getting rougher.'

'He seemed a nice enough kid. Of course that story could have been a bluff – first vandalize the library, then raise the alarm to give himself a sort of alibi. I mean, what was he doing, just staring out of the window? Sounds a bit thin to me.'

Bergerac shrugged. Teenagers could always find plenty of reasons for brooding in the night. So, for that matter, could adults. But Akbar seemed too old and too serious for a lad of his age. Too much in control. Bergerac made a mental note to check out his background. *If* he stayed on the case.

'Licensed boozing,' Goddard said enviously. 'It was never like that when I was at school. You want me to get Kim?'

Bergerac glanced at him. 'Yes. Let's get it over with. Barry . . . ?'

'What?'

'I want you to ask the questions, OK? Cover the obvious points. Then can you find a reason to leave us alone?'

The younger man nodded. If he was surprised, he concealed it well. It was unlike Bergerac to ask for family favours. Bergerac assured himself that it had sounded perfectly natural – a father wanting a private word with his daughter; even coppers were human.

Goddard tried to be tactful. He took Kim through the attack on her room, and through the argument in the dining hall beforehand. Kim refused point-blank to say why she had quarrelled with Chris Gunter. She avoided looking at her father while she was speaking. She huddled in her chair, prickly as a hedgehog and about as communicative.

'I don't know,' she kept saying in a wooden voice.

The expression on her face reminded Bergerac of the time, ten years earlier, when he had caught her with a stolen Mars Bar. But looking guilty wasn't the same as being guilty.

Goddard made a great show of looking at his watch. 'I'd better go and see if the lab reports have come in.'

'All right,' Bergerac said. 'See if you can find us some tea as well.'

Kim stood up, too. 'Is that all?'

'Not quite,' Bergerac said gently.

She sat down again, scowling. When Goddard had left, she looked at her father directly, for the first time that afternoon. 'Is this where you get the thumbscrews out?'

Her voice trembled as she spoke; the bravado was paper thin.

Bergerac said nothing. He allowed the silence to lengthen.

'I know what they're saying,' Kim said. 'They thing I'm the Prankster. You know something? I hate this place.'

'I don't go a bundle on it myself,' Bergerac said. 'Are you the Prankster?'

'Are you asking as a policeman?' she fired up. 'Or as my dad?'

'Answer the question, please.'

'You're not going to take my word for it. Why should I bother?'

She had a point. A policeman who believed everything he was told wouldn't last long in any force. And even parents couldn't afford to be credulous.

'Look, Kim – I know there are a lot of rumours flying around. That's inevitable in a place like this. But rumours don't concern me.'

'Right,' she said, standing up again. 'Great. That's it, is it?'

'Sit down. Are you the Prankster?'

She remained on her feet. 'No,' she said to the ceiling. 'Have we finished?'

Bergerac knew he was handling this badly. But he couldn't see another way to do it. She had decided he was hostile, and there was no way to change her mind. At present, he guessed, everyone seemed potentially hostile to her.

'We haven't finished,' Bergerac said harshly. 'I've got two pieces of evidence, both of which implicate you. I've made neither of them official. Not yet. I wanted to talk to you first.'

'*Evidence?*' Kim was a policeman's daughter: she knew the weight that was attached to the word. 'What do you mean?'

'I found this in your room a couple of hours ago.' Bergerac produced the sheet of newsprint and smoothed it out on the desk. For an instant her eyes met his; she understood the implications of the missing words and letters; and she was afraid. But how did she know about the newsprint format of the anonymous letters?

Then her head went back. 'So you've been prying, have you?' She sounded just like her mother. 'Where did you find it?'

'Between the bed and the wall.'

'I've never seen it before. But I suppose you won't believe that.'

'Have you had an anonymous letter yourself?'

She shook her head.

Bergerac touched the newspaper. 'Then how come you knew what this meant?'

'Everyone knows,' she said sullenly. 'Rose Wintersham had a letter like that, and so did Doncaster.'

It was plausible. Bergerac let the point go.

'Any idea how it could have got in your room?'

She shrugged. 'There's no lock on the door. Didn't you notice?'

So there it was: all he'd extracted from her was a straight, unhelpful denial. Unassailable, unless further evidence emerged. Forensic would have to analyse the sheet of paper for contact traces.

Bergerac switched his line of attack. 'I saw your grand-dad this morning.'

'Good for you.'

'You know that video tape you borrowed? *High Society*?'

She nodded; Bergerac could have sworn that she looked genuinely puzzled.

'He tried to play it back last night. But someone had switched the labels. He found himself watching a hard-porn movie.'

Kim giggled.

Bergerac, the memory of that obscenely sadistic film fresh in his mind, had to restrain himself from shouting at her.

'You gave the tape to your mother on Friday evening,' he said tightly.

'You think *she* switched the labels?'

'No. What I think, and what everyone else will think, is that the labels were switched while the tape was in your possession.'

'I can't stop you thinking.'

'Kim – just answer a few questions. I haven't got time for the funny stuff, OK? When did you get the tape?'

'Last weekend.'

'And where was it kept?'

'In my room. We had a meeting of the Film Club on Wednesday night, and I played some of it then. It was good for a few belly laughs. Afterwards it got left in the cupboard, with the other tapes and the VCR.'

'What cupboard?'

Kim sighed theatrically, as if she found the questions intolerably and unnecessarily wearisome. 'It's in a sort of function room, next to the Wintersham Library,' she explained. 'A lot of the smaller societies use it for meetings. And no, it's not locked. Anyone could have got in there.'

'All right,' Bergerac said. 'I've finished – unless there's anything you want to tell me?'

She shook her head. Then she said: 'I suppose you'll report them – the tape and the newspaper?'

Bergerac nodded.

Kim opened the door. 'Can't conceal *evidence*, can we?'

She left the office without saying goodbye.

Evidence? Circumstantial evidence – that was all it added up to. But even circumstantial evidence could be enough – especially in a case like this that was unlikely ever to come to court; Lady Wintersham, Hungerford and Upperwood would combine to prevent a prosecution. Kim's attitude hadn't helped. Bergerac had been hoping that she would come up with a cast-iron defence.

Goddard returned with a cup of tea. 'It's lukewarm by now,' he said. 'I didn't want to interrupt.'

He tactfully avoided asking how the interview had gone. Maybe Bergerac's face was all the answer he needed.

Bergerac took the tea and wandered across to the window.

'Farzanah was waiting outside for her,' Goddard said behind him in a neutral voice.

And there they were, Kim and Akbar, so close together that they were almost touching. They were walking across the grass towards the sixth-form centre. Kim was talking to him, waving her arms to emphasize what she was saying; and he was looking down at her and smiling.

Bergerac felt excluded.

'It's the first fire of the autumn,' Marcus said. 'Let's make toast.'

They knelt on the hearthrug, side by side and almost touching. Debby cut the bread; Marcus toasted it; she buttered it. They made far more than was necessary. Afterwards they sat on the floor, leaning against the big leather sofa. For a time, Debby succeeded in forgetting about Kim and that wretched video tape.

They were both pleasantly tired. After lingering over lunch they had gone for a walk along the cliffs. As the sun sank lower, the wind grew stronger; it was chilly enough to make the fire more than a luxury.

'So what do you think of it?' Marcus said, gesturing round the room,

'I'm surprised – I was expecting more bachelor squalor and less *Homes and Gardens*.'

It was the first time that Debby had been to Marcus's home; it marked, she felt, a new stage in their relationship. She had liked the sitting room immediately. Once, he told her, it had been a hayloft. It was a long, well-proportioned room, with the roof timbers and much of the stonework still exposed. He had rejected the obvious option of filling the place with antiques: the building was old, but everything inside it was modern; and for once the juxtaposition of old and new worked brilliantly.

Debby, who had an eye for interior design, knew that the furniture was mainly Swedish; the straight, clean lines and the preponderance of natural wood harmonized perfectly with the beams above their heads.

The wall opposite the fireplace was lined with shelves that housed the twin-deck video, the stereo system and scores of tapes and records. She could see only three pictures – none of them large but all of them well-placed and carefully lit. There was a Munch lithograph, a small Matisse and a Chagall.

Debby blinked. 'Are those originals?'

'I'm afraid so. Cost a fortune to insure. I inherited them from my father. He collected Expressionists.'

'I half expected you'd have your photographs up.'

He shook his head. 'In this company? I wouldn't dare. I've got some of mine in the study.'

The pictures represented a lot of money. Debby suddenly had the confidence to ask a question that had been in her mind for some time: 'Why do you work at Edward College? Surely you don't need to?'

'It's not a financial necessity. But I'm a trained accountant, and I have to do something. I can't just sit around all day, staring at Dad's pictures. It keeps me off the streets. Besides, I like the job. Not much money, but a lot of responsibility.'

His arm was lying along the seat of the sofa behind her. As he finished speaking, he moved it to her shoulders.

'I'm glad you're here.'

She snuggled closer to him. One of the things she liked about Marcus was his gentleness. He hadn't tried to force the pace. When he made a move, he always left her room to step back. They hadn't made love yet; but she thought they soon would. She was ready.

'Is there anything wrong?' he said softly. 'Sometimes today you've looked withdrawn. Worried, even.'

'Is it that obvious? I'm sorry.'

'Do you want to tell me?'

She hesitated, wanting to tell him but wondering if she should. Then it occurred to her that sooner or later he would probably hear about it from someone else. It was better that he should hear it from her first. After all, it concerned Kim.

'A problem shared,' Marcus said, 'is often a problem solved. Ancient Chinese proverb.'

It wasn't a good joke but it made her laugh and eased the tension she was feeling. She told him how *High Society* had somehow changed into a vicious hard-porn movie while the tape was in Kim's possession.

As she was speaking, she felt him becoming tenser. He took the matter much more seriously than she had expected. *Because he cares about me?* He asked several questions and soon extracted everything that her father had told her.

'Why the interest? Is it to do with this Prankster business?' She pulled away from him. 'You surely don't think that Kim – ?'

'No, of course not. But other people may. We have to face that.'

She was grateful for the 'we'. His face was sombre; she felt he was sharing her worry.

He glanced at her and smiled. 'Don't worry about it now,' he went on. 'Maybe that's a stupid thing to say. I've noticed that parents never stop worrying about their children, however old they are.'

'It's an occupational hazard,' Debby murmured.

'Take my aunt, for instance. You'd think nothing could worry her. But she's like a cat with one kitten where Rose is concerned. Though in her case there's some reason for it.'

'How do you mean?' Debby didn't particularly want to know; but she sensed that he was offering a confidence of his own in exchange for hers.

'Rose has always been wild. There was even an outbreak of petty thieving last term. My aunt called it kleptomania, of course — it sounds so much better than theft. She spent most of the summer taking Rose round a series of psychiatrists, to prove her point.'

'I had no idea . . .'

'It's not something my aunt wants to advertise. As you can imagine.'

Neither of them said anything for a moment. Debby was happy: Marcus had trusted her enough to tell her something mildly discreditable about his family. Her own difficulty no longer seemed quite so important.

'Debby? I . . . I sometimes think that one day I'd like children. Despite the worry.'

His arm tightened about her. She lifted her face. The kiss went on for a long time. Afterwards, there was no more conversation until the fire had burned down to a bed of glowing embers, and the last of the daylight had seeped away from the sky.

With a stab of panic, Theodore Poolstock realized that it was already dark outside. He had no idea it was so late.

He glanced down at the bound volume of speeches that commemorated the foundation ceremonies of Edward College, nearly fifty years before. He wasn't even halfway through.

The book was turning into a nightmare. There was so much work.

He stood up and drew the curtains. He was working at a small desk between two of the glass-fronted bookcases. The big table in the middle of the Old Library had been shrouded with dustsheets.

On the wall behind Lady Wintersham's chair was a discoloured rectangle of paint: the Sargent portrait of the Jersey Rose had been taken away by the police; Lady Wintersham had assured him that she would have it restored, if possible, in time for the jubilee. Poolstock shook his head: such a terrible, wanton act – verging on sacrilege.

A knock on the door made him start. His heart pounded. Surely the Prankster would not dare to return to the scene of his crime?

The door opened and the policeman looked into the room.

'I saw the light, sir,' he said. 'Just checking.'

'We live in terrible times, Sergeant er . . .'

'Bergerac. Will you be here long?'

'Sometimes I fear I shall be here for ever – there is so much to *do*.'

'I'll tell them downstairs.'

'Tell whom?'

'Constable Goddard and Mr Doncaster. They'll be patrolling the school at irregular intervals for the first part of the night. Another team will take over later.'

'I'm glad to hear it.'

'You haven't seen Mr Wintersham around today, have you? We've been trying to get hold of him.'

'Marcus? Yes, I saw him this morning, over at Heartland House. In fact he nearly ran me down.' Poolstock frowned at the memory. 'Or rather, that young woman of his did.'

The policeman, Poolstock fancied, was looking rather peculiar – almost strained. No doubt they had to work long hours. That was what they were paid for.

'Blonde?' Bergerac said. 'In her thirties? In a Mercedes?'

Poolstock nodded. 'They gave me a lift to school. And drove off *most* abruptly.'

'Did they say where they were going?'

'To play squash, I think. And possibly to take some photographs. Marcus had his camera case with him. It's a huge thing – I don't know what he puts in it. In my young day, I had a little box camera: it was perfectly adequate. But nowadays they have to have about four cameras and half a dozen lenses, and goodness only knows what. But they say he's very competent – I shall be asking his advice about the section of plates in the – '

'So you've no idea where they might be now?' Bergerac said with a touch of impatience.

'No, I'm afraid not,' Poolstock said tartly. 'Have you made any progress with that disgraceful letter?'

'Not yet. We're working on it.'

Poolstock sat down and picked up his pen. 'I wonder if you would excuse me, Sergeant? Fascinating though our conversation has been, I am really *very* busy.'

CHAPTER
12

When you're upset, your mind often abdicates its control over your actions; the vacuum is filled by a sort of automatic pilot composed of habit and instinct.

When Bergerac left Edward College, he had no clear idea of where he was going. He was barely aware that he was driving. All he knew was that he had to reach a decision about this case – and reach it soon.

He was off-duty now until tomorrow morning: that gave him a breathing space; but it was a mixed blessing, since it also gave him time to brood. The basic problem was that he had to cover the same ground both as a parent and as a copper: as a result he was failing dismally in both roles. He went over the day's events in his mind again and again, trying without success to find a scrap of comfort in them.

The Triumph, meanwhile, decided to take him home. Almost without warning, the little stone cottage loomed up in front of him. The headlights gave it a bleak, two-dimensional quality, like stage scenery. Bergerac turned off the engine and the lights. He realized with a jolt that he had no memory of the drive whatsoever.

The house was in darkness. When he went inside, the first thing that struck him was the dank, unlived-in smell of the place. He switched on the lights, blinking in the sudden glare, and looked round with the eyes of a stranger.

The open-plan layout mercilessly exhibited his private life. There was a pile of washing-up in the sink. A layer of dust carpeted the horizontal surfaces. A heap of bills and circulars waited for his attention on the kitchen table; they had been accumulating all week, waiting for the moment when he had the time and the money to deal with them. The bed was unmade and the sheets needed changing. The laundry basket was overflowing. The cottage wasn't a home: it was just a cage where problems lived; otherwise it was empty. He wanted to be somewhere else.

Bergerac made up his mind. He picked up the phone and punched in Crozier's home number. There was no point in putting it off. Delay would only make it worse. He would offer to go over to Crozier's house; this wasn't the sort of thing you could talk about on the phone. No, on second thoughts he wouldn't offer: he would insist. At least it would get him away from this damned cottage.

At the other end, the phone rang on and on. After a couple of minutes, Bergerac gave up. Barney and Alice must be out for the evening. But he needed to talk to someone.

He dialled another number. Susan had always complained that he didn't talk enough about his work. Maybe this would make up for it. Maybe something worth having would come out of this wretched affair.

The ringing stopped. 'Sue – ?'

There was a click as the answering machine turned itself on.

'No one's available to answer the phone at present,' Susan's voice said. 'Please leave your name and number after the bleep, and I will call you back as soon as possible. Unless you happen to be a policeman who spends his time in wine bars.'

Another click. A bleep.

Bergerac put down the phone and leant against the wall. For a long moment he stood there, wondering if he had just witnessed the final extinction of something that had been a long time dying. He was surprised to find that he no longer cared very much.

On impulse, he searched through the telephone directory for another number. Part of him hoped that there would be no answer. But the phone was answered on the second ring.

'Jenny?' His mouth was suddenly dry. 'This is Jim Bergerac.'

Goddard and Doncaster walked slowly up the main staircase. The broad landing was dimly illuminated by a single bulb. At the far end, there was a line of light under the door of the Old Library.

'He's still at it,' Doncaster said dryly. 'If perseverance is everything, it's going to be a brilliant book.'

'You have your doubts?'

Doncaster shrugged. 'Poolstock's one of those people who can't see the wood for the trees. As far as I can see, he's drowning himself in unnecessary detail.'

They walked along the landing, checking the offices on either side. On this floor, most of them belonged to the bursar and his staff. They didn't bother to turn on the lights – both men were carrying torches.

'If I were the Prankster,' Doncaster said, 'I'd lie low tonight. Apart from anything else, I'd need a good night's sleep.'

'I could do with some sleep myself,' Goddard said with a yawn.

He was grateful that chance had allocated Doncaster as his companion. The young master had served in the Royal Marines before he turned to teaching; he was a useful man to have around. He was also genuinely concerned about the welfare of the kids in his charge, which was more than could be said for his boss.

Doncaster nodded towards the Old Library. 'I imagine you'd feel happier if he was off the premises?'

'He's one more thing to worry about. We'd better look in on him.'

Poolstock was crouched over his desk, his nose only inches away from a book. As the door opened he glanced round. His eyes were red-rimmed. He looked both apprehensive and annoyed.

'Everything all right, sir?' Goddard said.

'I would be, if I didn't have to cope with these constant interruptions.'

'Will you be long?'

'Another quarter of an hour, perhaps.'

'You'll remember to lock up after you?'

'Of course.' Poolstock picked up his pen. 'Good night, Officer. Good night, James.'

They left him to it. The last port of call on their rounds was the sixth-form centre, where Doncaster had his rooms.

'I don't know about you,' Doncaster said as they walked across the grass, 'but I could do with a drink. I've got quite a nice malt whisky on the go. Are you allowed to join me?'

'I think,' Goddard said carefully, 'that in the circumstances I might be able to stretch a point.'

'There's something I'm missing,' Bergerac said for the second time. 'Something to do with old Poolstock.'

'Don't try to think about it,' Jenny said. 'Think of something else, and it'll pop out of the sub-conscious when you're not looking.'

He grinned. 'Easier said than done.'

They were still sitting in the kitchen of her bungalow. It was the first time he had been inside her home. As far as he could tell, it was furnished almost exclusively with books, some on shelves and others in piles on the floor. They were even in the hall and in the lavatory.

At the front door, she had taken one look at him and insisted on making him an omelette and a pot of coffee. He hadn't realized how hungry he was. There had been no time for lunch. He was aware that he had made a poor return for her hospitality – since his arrival he had talked almost non-stop, and mainly about himself and the case. She was a good listener, and she knew enough of the background to ask the right questions.

Crozier would have a fit if he ever discovered how much he had told Jenny. Confiding police business to shapely young women you barely knew was against all the rules.

Bergerac looked at her as she sat at the other end of the table, with her hands wrapped round a mug of coffee. There were no rings on her fingers – she was another survivor of a broken marriage. Tonight she hadn't dressed for seduction: she wore jeans and a fisherman's jersey; her hair was scraped back off her face and tied with a scrap of blue silk.

It occurred to him that for once he wasn't thinking of her sexually: he was thinking of her as a friend.

'It's two separate problems, really,' she said slowly. 'You're getting confused because your daughter's involved.'

'How do you mean?'

'You've got some circumstantial evidence that suggests that Kim might be the Prankster. I don't think you've got any choice there: you've got to report it. But frankly I don't think it's worth much. She'd have known the tape would be traced back to her. And finding that newspaper in her room was just too easy. If the Prankster is that stupid, he or she would have been caught out weeks ago. I'd lay you ten to one that someone's trying to frame her.'

It was a relief to hear her say it. Someone outside the case, who wasn't involved with Edward College or the States Police. Someone who, in her own field, was expert at assessing evidence.

'Who's got a down on her?' Jenny went on. 'That's where I'd begin. What about the American boy?'

'Chris Gunter? I wish I could find out why they quarrelled.'

'Maybe it was about you.'

'Me? Why?'

'Just an idea. You'd turned up at Edward College yesterday morning. And the graffito on Kim's mirror was something about piglets, wasn't it?'

'Just the one word – PIGLET.'

'Well, there you are. It's an obvious swipe at you.'

She was right – and he ought to have realized the possible significance of that before.

'So let's leave Kim out of it,' Jenny said. 'What have we got left?'

'Three things.' Bergerac counted them off on his fingers. 'Yves killed at Mont Desir. The Prankster. And that snuff movie, which might have something to do with hard porn coming through Jersey in quantity. But they don't necessarily tie up.'

'We know that Yves was investigating Edward College, the Jersey Rose and cocaine use at the time of his death. The Prankster's at Edward College. It's a reasonable inference that the sending of the tape to Hungerford was the Prankster's work; it's all of a piece with the other things. And it's too much of a coincidence to assume that there are two sources of hard porn, so the Prankster must be involved with that racket, too. Or at least have access to it.'

'It's all theory.' Bergerac knew he sounded ungracious. 'And it doesn't get us very far, either.'

'I don't know. If I were you, I'd concentrate on Edward College.'

'It's unlikely I'll be concentrating on anything for much longer. If I don't resign, they'll probably push me off the case.'

'Mr Grumpy,' Jenny said. Her mouth twitched.

Despite himself, Bergerac grinned back. He had to admit

that he was feeling better – partly because of the food and sympathy, but more because the case no longer seemed so unmanageable with Kim out of the way.

Jenny seemed to sense his change of mood. 'Why don't we do something about it? Now?'

'Like what? I can't very well go back to the school. Especially not with you.' He smiled. 'Sorry – I didn't put that very tactfully.'

'But there's no reason why we shouldn't go out for a drink. As long as you don't mind being seen with me in public.'

He caught her meaning at once. 'The Golden Ball?'

'It's an idea, isn't it? It's obviously a sort of sixth-form local. And Yves thought there might be a connection with the cocaine.'

'It's CID territory now,' Bergerac objected half-heartedly. 'The drug squad won't like me muscling in.'

'But it's still open to the public.' She pushed back her chair. 'Anyway, you're so restless that if you don't do something soon, you'll explode. I don't want a mess in my kitchen.'

Their eyes met. Bergerac nodded. Almost anything was better than sitting around and waiting for Barney Crozier to answer his phone. There was one alternative to going out: he could see it in her eyes, and he guessed it was reflected in his own. But this wasn't the right time for either of them. Not yet.

'Good,' she said briskly. 'I'll go and get changed.'

Theodore Poolstock took off his glasses and rubbed his eyes.

If he left now, he would be in time to catch the last bus to St Helier. He returned the volume to its place on the shelves and relocked the bookcase. It had been an infuriating day, on balance – all those interruptions had ruined his concentration beyond repair.

He shuffled his notes together, making sure they were in order, and put them in his briefcase. His papers were always getting disorganized: it was most annoying. Again he blamed the interruptions from the police – they were so confusing.

Still, it was reassuring to know that the authorities were at least taking the problem seriously. He doubted if he would have spent the evening here if he hadn't known that the school was being patrolled.

Before he left, he opened the curtains. By Upperwood's orders, all the outside lights were on. There were still great patches of darkness in the grounds of Edward College, but Poolstock was sure he would be able to avoid them. Fortunately, the drive was especially well-lit. There was nothing to worry about.

He closed the door of the Old Library, locking it carefully behind him; Lady Wintersham had arranged for him to have a set of keys. Suddenly he felt very tired. The journey back to his little flat seemed impossibly arduous. He was no longer a young man. More than anything he would have liked to be in his own chair by his own fire.

To cap it all, his rheumatism was playing up. The twinges usually signalled a change in the weather. Perhaps they had seen the last of the Indian summer.

He walked slowly down the uncarpeted landing His heels echoed against the highly varnished oak boards. Once or twice he glanced behind him, convinced that someone was following in his footsteps. That was mere foolishness, he chided himself, brought on by tiredness. He passed portraits of former headmasters, most of whom he had known. Now why hadn't the Prankster attacked *them*? Perhaps they were next on the list. He shivered.

When he reached the head of the stairs, he paused to

regain his breath. Dr Fender had warned him to take it easy after the heart attack last year. No more running for buses; no more unnecessary strain. Not for the first time, he wondered if he had been foolish to accept the Jersey Rose commission. For an instant he was tempted to withdraw. Then common sense prevailed. He had already spent much of the commission. And people would think it odd if he suddenly decided not to write the book. They would laugh behind his back. They would say he was past it.

He shifted the briefcase to his other hand and took a firm grip on the banisters. It didn't really matter if he missed the bus. He could always hang the expense and phone for a taxi.

Behind him, a door closed softly.

Poolstock gasped. His hand tightened convulsively on the banister. A sharp pain lanced through his chest and was gone.

There were footsteps behind him. Real footsteps – not echoes.

He let go of the rail and turned round slowly. Automatically, he raised the briefcase – an ineffectual shield but the only one he had.

'Oh,' he said breathlessly, 'it's you.' The relief was almost as intolerable as the fear had been. 'I thought . . . I don't know what I thought . . .'

The footsteps came closer.

Something was wrong, Poolstock realized abruptly. He saw a frown where he expected a smile.

'Has something happened?' he said, speaking so fast that the words were barely intelligible. 'Were you looking for me?'

The heel of the hand shot forward and caught him squarely in the chest. Poolstock fell backwards. He tried to regain his balance but the ground was six inches lower than it should have been.

The toe of his right foot touched the tread of a stair. He overbalanced completely, pitching backwards down the staircase.

Suddenly the pain returned. This time it radiated across his chest and spread to his neck. He was falling, falling.

This is death, he thought, quite calmly, despite the intensity of the pain. *So this is what it's like.*

His body landed at a forty-five-degree angle, head downwards, on the stairs. The briefcase followed another route: as he fell backwards, Poolstock had lost his grip on it; it flew over the banisters and fell with a thud in the hall beneath.

Poolstock's body slithered a few feet down the stairs.

The impact of the fall had forced open the lock of the briefcase. Once again, Poolstock's papers were in confusion.

CHAPTER
13

The first person they saw in the Golden Ball had no right to be there.

The pub had once been a pleasant nineteenth-century inn. It straggled round three sides of a yard. Successive owners had done their best to drag it screaming into the twentieth century. In its present incarnation, the exterior was rendered with pebbledash, painted yellow and draped with strings of coloured lights.

'Like a dowager with rows of plastic pearls,' Jenny Godly said appreciatively.

Bergerac reversed the Triumph into one of the few spaces left outside. As the engine died, the thud of the music became audible. They were playing an old Status Quo number, one of the disco standards that never seemed to die.

Big glass doors led into a foyer. Then the customer had a choice: to turn left into what had once been a barn or stabling, for the delights of the disco; or right, into a more orthodox bar, which also served food. Leaning in the doorway of the latter, glass in hand, was Rose Wintersham.

She saw Bergerac as soon as he saw her. She was dressed in jeans and short leather jacket. Her first reaction was to try to conceal the glass behind her; her second was to try the effect of a smile.

It was the sort of situation that Bergerac loathed – not just because of the unwanted reminder that a policeman is never off-duty, but also because it made him feel like a petty tyrant. But he had no choice: such encounters were part of the job.

He moved across the foyer towards the bar. Rose looked assessingly at Jenny, as if at a potential rival.

'I don't think you should be here,' Bergerac said softly.

'I'm with someone who's eighteen,' she said. 'Honest.'

'Maybe – but you're sixteen. And I don't think that's a soft drink you've got there.'

Rose grinned at him. 'All right, Holmes: it's a fair cop. It's Southern Comfort, actually.'

The words hardly mattered: the girl's indefinable charm did. Ignoring Jenny, she beamed it on Bergerac. Despite himself, he grinned back.

'You're not going to shop me, are you?' she asked. 'My mother would murder me.'

In theory, he knew, he should bring down the whole majesty of the law on Rose Wintersham. In practice, it just wasn't worth it. Besides, it would ruin his evening. He had no intention of spending the next few hours fending off an outraged Lady Wintersham. He held out his hand for the glass. Rose swallowed the rest of its contents before she surrendered it.

'You'd better get back to school. Now.'

'You're a darling, Sergeant.'

Jenny snorted with suppressed laughter.

'I'm not going to report you this time,' Bergerac said, trying without much success to keep his voice stern. 'But don't try it again, OK? I'll have to have a word with the manager.'

'Prevention is better than cure,' she said. 'Tell you what. One good turn deserves another. I'll pass the word round.'

'You do that. How will you get back? Do you need a lift?'

Rose glanced at Jenny. 'No, I'll walk,' she said with a sniff. 'It's not far. See you.'

With perfect self-possession, she walked across the foyer to the door, waggling her bottom for Bergerac's benefit.

When they were alone, Jenny said, 'You do realize that I probably saved your virtue just then? She'd have eaten you alive if you'd been by yourself. She certainly wouldn't have turned down a cosy ride *à deux* in your Noddy car. Who is she?'

Bergerac explained. 'I suppose I'd better drop a word in Upperwood's ear,' he said finally. 'Advise him to put the Golden Ball off-limits. That man's a fool.'

'Is having a date with a copper always like this?' Jenny asked. 'A never-ending mix of business and pleasure?'

'I'm afraid the pleasure tends to be optional,' Bergerac said. 'That's what Susan used to say.'

Jenny nodded, understanding – and apparently accepting – what he didn't want to put into words: *If you take me, you take my job*. She led the way through the crowd of drinkers to the bar, where she ordered a glass of wine for herself and a Perrier for him. Bergerac tried to pay, but she told him not to be so sexist.

Bergerac leant across the bar and flashed his warrant card discreetly at the young man who had served them. He had two studs in his left ear and a bad case of acne.

'I'd like a word with the manager.'

The barman twitched like a startled rabbit and scuttled away.

A moment later, he returned with Detective Sergeant Doug McCann.

It was an awkward moment for everyone – the barman, who was young enough to consider the police to be his natural enemies; Jenny, who sensed that something was wrong; Bergerac, who suspected he had put his foot in it; and McCann, who looked on the verge of tears.

McCann recovered first. He lifted the flap in the counter

153

and joined them on the other side of the bar. He steered Bergerac and Jenny into the relative privacy of the foyer.

'What are *you* doing here, Jim?' he said despondently. 'Didn't you see my memo?'

Bergerac shook his head. 'I've not been into the office today.'

His suspicion hardened into certainty: he had blundered into a drug-squad operation.

McCann propped himself against the nearest wall, as though the weight of his body was no longer a burden he was able to support. 'The owners are cooperating nicely. I'm temporary assistant under-manager for the evening. Uniformed branch will seal all exits in a few minutes. Then we go in with a fine-tooth comb.'

'I'm sorry, Doug. I didn't know.'

'It's the old, old story: the Bureau *never* liaise with CID. Why did you want the manager?'

'I've just sent home an underage drinker. Rose Wintersham, from Edward College.'

McCann's face didn't exactly brighten, but it became a fraction less gloomy. 'Lady Wintersham's daughter? *She* was here? Maybe it's just as well you came.'

He didn't have to spell it out: the trouble with blanket drug busts was that you tended to turn up a host of irrelevant minor misdemeanors. An underage drinker with an influential mother would be a waste of everyone's time and energy.

'Um,' McCann said, staring inquisitively and with a complete lack of embarrassment at Jenny. 'But why exactly did you come here in the first place?' He waved a limp hand at their surroundings. 'I wouldn't have thought this was your usual choice for an evening out.'

'Yves,' Bergerac said. 'Edward College. Testing the waters.'

McCann glanced at Jenny.

'It's OK, Doug. Dr Godly knows.' Bergerac realized he had made a mistake: by tomorrow, the news that he had confided in an outsider would have circulated round CID and probably reached the Bureau. He tried to retrieve himself: 'She's a sort of . . . expert witness.'

'I see.' McCann's eyes glinted.

'Do you want us to go?'

McCann nodded. 'It might be better. If you – '

The door to the disco bar opened and the rest of McCann's words were drowned by a surge of music. A tall young man with red hair was standing in the doorway with his back to them.

'Come on,' he shouted, so loudly that they could hear him above the music. 'We've got to go.'

He turned, and Bergerac glimpsed familiar features that were twisted with urgency.

It was Chris Gunter.

The recognition was mutual. Gunter broke into a run. As he passed Jenny, he shoved her towards Bergerac, who was already moving to intercept him. He would have reached the doors if McCann had not stretched out his right leg.

Gunter tripped and sprawled on the carpet.

The music stopped in mid-bar. The public-address system came to life: 'This is a police announcement . . .'

The doors opened from the outside. Two uniformed constables looked down at Gunter.

McCann shook his head, more in sorrow than in anger. 'Some people never learn,' he said to Bergerac, 'do they?'

The shortest route to Edward College was over the fields. But it was a dark night, and Rose decided to go back by road.

After a couple of hundred yards, she began to wish that she had accepted the copper's offer of a lift. Her mind ran ahead: it would be difficult when she got back to school — everyone would be on the alert for the Prankster. There were rumours that the police were going to patrol the place during the night.

But she would manage somehow. You could always find a way.

A car was approaching from the direction of the school. Its headlights were on full-beam. Rose tried to duck off the road — it might be a teacher or even someone from Heartland House — but a wall prevented her. As it drew nearer, the car slowed. She shoved her hands in her pockets and waited. If necessary she would claim that she had Upperwood's permission; he wouldn't want a row. You could always find a way if you tried hard enough.

The car stopped. The window rolled down.

'Hallo, Rose.'

What a piece of luck, she thought. *The one person who has to do what I want.*

'Can I give you a lift back to school?'

'Yes,' she said. 'I'd like that.'

'I'm sorry,' Bergerac said again, 'but I think you'd better go. I called a taxi for you.'

Jenny Godly looked up at him. 'I don't think I've ever had such an interesting date.'

'You're not angry?'

'If you don't take anything for granted, you don't get hurt.' Suddenly her face was bleak. 'That's my theory, anyway.'

'I don't know how long this'll take. Shall I give you a call if it's not too late?'

'If you want . . . Damn it, Jim, give me a call whenever it is. OK?'

The taxi arrived. She kissed him quickly on the cheek. Bergerac went back into the pub. McCann was in the manager's office; he was in the process of organizing a convoy to take them to police headquarters. He waved Bergerac to a chair and finished his conversation on the phone.

Afterwards, the first thing he said was, 'Has your young lady gone?'

Bergerac nodded, not bothering to explain that Jenny wasn't his young lady, and probably never would be. 'How's it going?'

The net result of the raid was encouraging, McCann said – in a melancholy manner that suggested that his mother had recently died – but not exactly sensational. Six people, five male and one female; all under twenty, none of them from Edward College; and each with half a gram of cocaine concealed about their persons. There was one oddball – a thirty-year-old accountant-cum-weekend-hippy, discovered in the gents with a quarter-ounce of Lebanese Red tucked in his left sock – who was irrelevant to McCann's present investigation but a useful addition to the arrest statistics. And Chris Gunter. Eight arrests. Small beer but, all in all, it was a good evening's work.

Gunter had been carrying several hundred pounds in cash and five sachets, each containing half a gram of cocaine.

'He recognized one of my DCs in the disco, and he panicked,' McCann said disapprovingly. 'If he'd had any sense, he'd have tried to flush the coke down the toilet.'

'You'll be charging him?' Bergerac said. 'They'll probably try and stop you.'

'Too bad,' McCann murmured.

'Does Upperwood know?'

'The Headmaster? Yes, he's meeting us at Rouge Bouillon. We're doing this one by the book.'

'Doug – do me a favour: let me sit in on the interview.'

157

'Um.' McCann's face lengthened. 'On one condition. You keep your mouth shut.'

Nigel Upperwood found it difficult to concentrate on what the policeman was saying. His attention was split between three misfortunes: first the Prankster, then Virginia's defection and now his terrible disappointment over Chris Gunter.

Oddly enough, it was Virginia's refusal to return to Edward College that hurt him the most. Being irritated with her had become a habit: he missed not having her around.

He forced himself to listen.

'. . . how long has this been going on?' Sergeant McCann asked.

The interview room was silent. Gunter stared down at the red carpet tiles on the floor; physically, he was the largest person in the room, but he looked somehow deflated. In one corner, Sergeant Bergerac was examining his nails. By the door, a young constable turned over a page in his notebook, licked his pencil and looked up expectantly.

McCann sighed and answered his own question. 'At least since May. We've independent evidence on that. You do realize that it's in your own interests to cooperate?'

Gunter lifted his head. 'I want a lawyer.'

'You can have one,' McCann said. 'It won't make any difference. You were caught with the stuff on you. Six witnesses confirm you were selling, and that they've bought from you in the past. You resisted arrest.'

'Can't you do something?' Gunter said to Upperwood.

The headmaster cleared his throat. 'The school solicitor is on his way.' This business had gone too far to be hushed up. 'I – ah – I would advise you to make a clean breast of it, Chris.'

'You really want me to talk?'

'Of course I do. Honesty is always the best policy.'

'You're crazy.'

Upperwood was deeply disappointed in Gunter. The boy had seemed such a caring, politically committed individual – an ideal person to act as an advertisement for the educational ethos of Edward College. Now it seemed he was no more than a trainee capitalist with criminal inclinations.

'Why crazy?' McCann asked with sudden interest.

Gunter said nothing.

'Because of what else might come out?' McCann leant forward across the table. 'You're finished – you do realize that? You've got no way out. The only choice you've got is between bad and worse. If you're sensible, you'll cooperate and we'll make things as easy as possible. If you go on being stupid, a lot of people are going to regret it, especially your parents. But yourself most of all, I can promise you that.'

Gunter still refused to reply. Upperwood opened his mouth, intending to urge the boy to be sensible; but McCann stopped him with a frown.

Then Upperwood realized why there was no need for him to speak. Gunter's shoulders were shaking. The macho shell was so thin that it shattered under pressure. The boy put his head on his arms and began to cry.

McCann gave him a moment. Then he said, 'Now, Chris. I want to know where you got the stuff, how you brought it in, where you keep it, and who's buying it. Let's start at the beginning.'

Gunter lifted his head. Tears glistened incongruously on his blunt-featured face. 'OK,' he said in a whine that contrasted strongly with the aggressive drawl he had used before. 'But don't tell Mom.'

*

She could have sworn that a light moved against one of the darkened windows in the old house.

She waited. Nothing else happened. The window was dark again. It was in what had once been the kitchen wing. Now the wing housed the art department and several craft workshops.

Maybe she had imagined the light.

Kim, who was sitting on the end of her bed, rocked to and fro. She had switched off her own light hours ago, and hadn't bothered to draw the curtains. The incident penetrated the numbness in her mind. The numbness had been building up all day, as they had tried and condemned her in her absence. Everyone, even her father, seemed convinced that she was the Prankster. Everyone except Akbar.

Suppose there had been a light – a torch perhaps? Suppose it was the Prankster?

There was a rumour that police and certain members of staff were patrolling the school tonight – it might have been them. On the other hand . . .

She swung her legs off the bed and pulled on jeans and a jersey over her pyjamas. There was no harm in making sure. She pushed her feet into a pair of trainers and hurriedly laced them up. It seemed that no one else was going to clear her, so she had to help herself.

She opened her door and padded along the corridor and up the stairs to Doncaster's rooms. He was the sixth-form tutor who was meant to be on duty. To her relief, there was a line of light under the door. She knocked and waited, but there was no answer.

The door was unlocked. She put her head inside the room. It was empty. On the coffee table there were two glasses and a bottle of whisky. She went across to the window. Two men were walking over the lawn. Even at this distance Kim could recognize Doncaster's broad back. They vanished into a patch of shadow beneath a cedar.

On patrol?

Simultaneously, the realization hit her that, if he was on patrol in the grounds, it couldn't have been Doncaster shining a torch in the house. If there *had* been a torch.

She left the room and ran downstairs and out of the building. The night air was unexpectedly chilly. She hesitated for an instant in the doorway. The school had become an unfamiliar patchwork of light and dark. Anyone could be lurking in the shadows. Suddenly she wanted company very badly. She was tempted to go back and wake Akbar; but the more she delayed, the greater the risk of losing the Prankster.

The only thing to do was to follow Doncaster. Suddenly reckless, she sprinted across the grass towards the cedar. The risk of alerting the Prankster ruled out the possibility of shouting. As she reached the tree, she heard the click of a door closing, somewhere in the old house.

Of course – they would patrol inside as well as outside.

Kim ran on. She guessed the sound had come from the back door that gave access to the art department.

The guess seemed confirmed when she tried the door and found that it was unlocked. Inside there were a few lights burning along the corridor that led to the hall at the front of the house. She walked quietly along it, listening for footsteps.

The great house was silent around her. Naturally, she told herself, Doncaster wouldn't want to make a noise. Kim began to regret what she was doing. She should have woken Akbar or found a phone; at any rate she should have stayed in the safety of the sixth-form centre.

Safety? Nowhere in Edward College was safe from the Prankster.

She reached the hall. It was empty, and all the doors that gave on to it were shut. A briefcase was lying on the floor, surrounded by a mess of papers.

Then Kim glanced at the dimly lit stairs.

Her mind refused to accept what she saw. It was just a trick of the light. It was a few old clothes that someone had dropped. She'd fallen asleep on her bed and was having a nightmare. Her stomach churned.

She shook herself like a dog emerging from water. It was no use fooling herself. The man was lying on his back, head downwards, with the face turned away from her.

But Kim recognized the tweed jacket.

She forced her legs to obey her and climbed the stairs. It was Poolstock, no doubt about it; a stupid old man, but he didn't deserve this. She had to know if he was dead or alive. Her whole body trembled, and she was sobbing almost soundlessly.

He can't be dead.

Kim bent down so she could see the face. It was then that she screamed.

The face was suffused with blood beneath the skin. It was inhuman. She didn't want to look at it. Automatically she pulled herself backwards.

She missed the step; indeed, she had forgotten she was on the stairs at all. She fell backwards, her arms flailing.

Then something hit her with blinding force just above her ear. A split second later, a jolt went through her body – through the entire world.

Darkness enveloped her, and she welcomed it.

CHAPTER
14

McCann, three of his men and a sniffer dog called Zonk went through the sixth-form centre like a dose of salts through an unruly digestive system.

Upperwood tagged along for the ride, accompanied by another master, in his dressing-gown, and a sturdy little matron with button eyes and a pursed mouth. At first the headmaster was in a talkative mood: the need for discretion was one theme; another was what Lady Wintersham might say and do. But as time passed, even Upperwood grew silent.

When Gunter had finally cracked, he couldn't stop talking. Among the information he gave them was one location and four names. The drug-squad team soon flushed out fourteen grams of Colombian cocaine, hidden in a rain-water tank on the flat roof, the residue of the twenty-five grams he had imported from Miami in September. They found three of Gunter's customers, two of them in the same bed. They also picked up another gram and a half of cocaine.

But the fourth customer, Rose Wintersham, wasn't in her room, though they did discover a tin-opener with a plastic handle. If you prised open the top of the handle, you found a cylindrical cavity inside. This one contained half a gram of coke and a rather smaller amount of Chinese heroin. As Gunter had told them, she used to smoke the heroin in joints: the tobacco, matches and cigarette papers were concealed in a hollowed-out book, along with a razor blade for chopping up the cocaine. Druggies, McCann observed, thought the hiding places they dreamed up were original, but usually they had the same ideas as other druggiees; it made his job so much easier.

While they were in Rose's room they made another, equally interesting discovery that had nothing to do with drugs: a pair of fine rubber gloves, the kind surgeons wear, was hidden between the carpet and the underlay; one of the fingertips was smudged with white gloss paint.

McCann searched every room in the place, waking up most of the sixth form as he did so. He didn't find Rose but he did find another empty room: Kim Bergerac's.

Bergerac, meanwhile, was briefing Goddard and Doncaster on what had happened, in the latter's sitting room. He tactfully ignored the two glasses beside the whisky bottle. They left him to resume their patrol of the school, leaving him kicking his heels and wondering how Crozier would react to this unauthorized and impromptu cooperation between the Bureau and CID. McCann found him there and broke the news that Kim had disappeared. Suddenly Crozier became the least of Bergerac's worries.

He phoned Debby straight away, using Doncaster's phone, to see if Kim had gone home. Kim wasn't there, but Debby announced her intention of driving over to the school immediately. There was no sign of panic in her voice, which did not surprise him: Debby had an unexpected talent for remaining calm in a real crisis; temperamental outbursts were reserved for day-to-day annoyances like a disobedient child or a husband who never got home from work on time.

While Bergerac was talking to her, the little sitting room filled up with policemen and staff. The headmaster arrived last of all. His face twitched uncontrollably; his voice had risen in pitch and lost the precise enunciation that it usually had.

'We'll have to search the whole school,' McCann said with ghoulish pleasure. 'I've radioed for reinforcements.'

'Is that really necessary?' Upperwood bleated. He eyed the bottle on the table. 'Haven't you enough men already?'

'Can't take any chances, sir. I'm sure Sergeant Bergerac would agree.'

Bergerac nodded curtly.

'And I think you'd better inform Miss Wintersham's mother,' McCann went on. 'Just in case.'

Upperwood winced. He poured himself a shot of Doncaster's whisky and swallowed it in seconds. Then he tried to phone Marcus Wintersham.

'So much better if a member of the family breaks the news to her,' he murmured to no one in particular.

But the phone rang unanswered at the old coach-house, and Upperwood was forced to contact Lady Wintersham himself. The connection was good; everyone else in the room pretended not to listen to the short, explosive conversation that ensued.

Everyone except Bergerac. *Marcus Wintersham*. He wasn't where everyone expected him to be. An idea slipped into Bergerac's mind; it was an unwelcome visitor, because at present only Kim mattered and he couldn't cope with distractions. Nevertheless the thought lodged there. He had to talk to Theodore Poolstock: it all depended on what the old man said. But it would have to wait – tonight the parent took precedence over the policeman.

Itching at the delay, he discussed the details of the search with McCann, who refused to be hurried.

'We'll need a plan of the school, sir,' McCann said to Upperwood.

'There's one in the bursar's office, in the old house. Where *is* Marcus? He's never around when one wants him.'

'We'll organize the search from there,' Bergerac said. 'It's more central.'

The whole party left the sixth-form centre. On the stairs they were joined by Akbar Farzanah.

'Go back to your room,' Upperwood snapped.

Akbar just looked at him.

'He might be useful,' Bergerac said. 'He knows the layout.'

More to the point, he was thinking, Akbar knew Kim – perhaps better, in one sense, than her own parents did.

Just as they reached the lawn, the front door of the old house opened and James Doncaster emerged. He waved at them, shouted something and ran over the grass towards them.

What Doncaster said was drowned by the roar of two cars coming up the drive, bumper to bumper. A Mercedes and an Aston Martin: two determined mothers, hurrying to protect their young.

Bergerac broke into a sprint, with Akbar close behind. They almost collided with Doncaster under the big cedar.

'We've found Kim,' the teacher said, gasping for breath. 'She's unconscious, but I think she's OK.' He laid a hand on Bergerac's arm to detain him. 'I'm afraid there's more. Ted Poolstock's lying on the stairs. He's dead.'

It was a strange moment to discover that you liked your ex-wife.

'I wish to God the ambulance would come,' Debby said. 'I wish . . .' She relapsed into silence.

Kim had been moved to a sofa in the hall. Fender, the school doctor, had already examined her. There was a bruise above and slightly behind one ear. When Goddard and Doncaster found her, she was lying diagonally across the stairs, several yards below Poolstock's body. It looked as if she had hit her head on the sharp corner at the base of the banisters.

She was very pale, and her skin was clammy. Her pulse

was fast and weak, and her breathing shallow. Nevertheless, Fender thought there was nothing to worry about. It was just a matter of time before she came round.

Just a matter of time . . . Minutes? Hours? Days?

And it was just a matter of time before they knew what had happened. Had Poolstock fallen or had he been pushed? Fender had mentioned that the old man had a weak heart. Accident or murder? Was Kim responsible? They were still no nearer to the identity of the Prankster.

Debby and Bergerac were crouching by the sofa, so close that their arms touched. Akbar hovered a few yards away, tactfully out of earshot; he had resisted all attempts to send him back to his room. Around them, the search went on.

'Jim, she'll be all right, won't she?'

'Of course she will.' He tried to smile at her. 'Kim's always been tough. Remember the time she fell down the stairs at our old cottage? On to a stone floor?'

There was a long, oddly companionable silence. Both of them were watching Kim's face, willing her eyelids to open.

'Do you know where Marcus is?' Debby whispered.

Both of them were talking in whispers, despite the noise of tramping feet around them. Lady Wintersham was trying to direct the search; McCann was doggedly ignoring her.

'No . . . Upperwood tried to phone him at the coach-house but there was no answer.'

'It's odd.' Debby sounded disconsolate.

'You saw him today?' Bergerac asked. 'Poolstock mentioned something about seeing you.'

'We spent the whole day together – until about seven o'clock.' There was a slight flush on Debby's fair skin. 'Then I had to get back for one of Dad's dinners, and Marcus said he had some work to do.'

Something in her voice betrayed her: this had been a special day for her. Bergerac felt like a heel but he couldn't afford to spare her feelings. Not now, when there was a possibility that Poolstock's death had not been an accident. *And Kim might be mixed up in it.*

'At home or at school?' he said.

'He didn't say.'

'What happened when you met Poolstock? What did you talk about?'

'Does it matter?' Debby said angrily. 'It's Kim we should be concerned about.'

Bergerac touched her hand. 'Trust me. It could be important for all of us. Kim, too.'

She glanced at him, suddenly interested. 'But it was nothing, really. Poolstock had fallen over in the drive at Heartland House, tripped over a stone or something. We picked him up and gave him a lift here. Nearly got nabbed by Lady Wintersham.'

'But what did you talk about?'

Debby shrugged. 'He was going to work in the Old Library, I remember that. We mentioned squash. He went on about the new services in the school chapel since Upperwood went over. Oh yes, and he asked Marcus to help with the photographs for his book.'

'How did that come about?'

Debby's eyes had returned to Kim. 'Poolstock saw Marcus's camera case on the back seat,' she said mechanically. But she wasn't being unhelpful: talking about anything was better than thinking about Kim. 'It's one of those big, black-leather jobs that holds everything including the kitchen sink. Poolstock thought he'd seen Marcus with a metal case.'

Bergerac felt a surge of excitement: it ran through him like a flash of electricity.

'Marcus said he had two, I think,' Debby continued, 'though I've only seen him with the black leather one. I wasn't paying much attention. I got the impression that

Poolstock thought that so much equipment was all a waste of money.'

He had the final connection. A few facts, tied together with shreds of speculation, made a circuit in his mind. It was just a theory – no more than that; unproven and, now Poolstock was dead, possibly unprovable.

Debby was looking at him curiously. 'What is it?' Her voice rose. 'Is it something about Marcus? You've got to tell me.'

Kim moaned and opened her eyes. Frowning slightly, she glanced first at Debby, then at Bergerac. She looked away, her eyes focusing on someone who was behind them. Her lips trembled, and then shaped themselves into a weak smile. A smile of relief.

'Akbar,' she said.

They were looking at him with something closely akin to pity in their eyes. All of them – Doug McCann, Barry Goddard, Upperwood, James Doncaster and Lady Wintersham. Even Lady Wintersham.

'She remembers *nothing* after that?' Lady Wintersham's disbelief was obvious from her tone. 'How unfortunate, Sergeant.'

'Dr Fender says it's quite normal,' Bergerac said, 'Memory of the injury is usually absent after you're stunned. Sometimes there's more memory loss.'

'Still,' McCann said sadly, 'it's a pity.'

So some of them still wanted Kim to be the Prankster – caught at the scene of the crime. It would be so convenient. It might even help to divert attention from the uncomfortable fact that Lady Wintersham's daughter was into hard drugs. But they hadn't the guts to put it into words. Not yet. Bergerac nearly mentioned the rubber gloves that had been found in Rose's room. They could wait: it all depended on what forensic came up with in the way of fingerprints.

'The last thing she remembers is seeing a light in the Art Department and looking for you' – he nodded at Doncaster – 'and Goddard.'

No one said anything. It seemed to Bergerac that the silence was full of unspoken accusations. Anger stirred in him. What right had they to judge?

They were standing in the bursar's office, which had become the unofficial headquarters of the operation. Debby and Kim were still downstairs, waiting for the overdue ambulance. According to McCann, Barney Crozier should be on his way to Edward College; he had been given overall control. Maybe Barney was a potential ally.

'Well, this is all very interesting,' Lady Wintersham said, 'but I want to find Rose.'

Bergerac finally lost his temper. 'Then look for your nephew. I reckon they're together.'

'I *beg* your pardon? Perhaps you would care to explain yourself.'

It was not an easy request to deal with. Bergerac already regretted what he had said. A theory, however plausible, was not the sort of thing that would satisfy Lady Wintersham in her present mood.

'Mr Marcus Wintersham?' McCann interrupted unexpectedly. 'What sort of a car's he got?'

Lady Wintersham turned her frown on him. 'A black Audi. Though I fail to see what – '

'There's a black Audi in one of the staff garages,' McCann said simply. 'So he may well be here.'

'But that's impossible. You'd have found him. Or he would have come out to see what all the fuss was about. I imagine he walked home.'

'But we haven't found him,' Bergerac said softly. 'He hasn't come out to see what all the fuss is about. He's not at home either. So where is he?'

'Well, he's not here – '

'He's the bursar,' Bergerac went on relentlessly. 'He probably knows the school buildings better than anyone. And we still haven't explained the light that Kim saw in the Art Department.'

Doncaster coughed with uncharacteristic diffidence. 'I wonder . . . Has anyone tried the cellars?'

'What cellars?' Bergerac snapped. 'Under here?'

'Cellars?' Upperwood said. 'I didn't know we had any.'

'They're under the kitchen wing,' Doncaster said. 'In other words, under the Art Department. No one uses them – they're too damp. One of the kids broke his leg down there a few years back, so we blocked up the entrance.'

'Then we'd better check it's still blocked,' Bergerac said.

'Preposterous,' Lady Wintersham said. But she followed them out of the room.

Doncaster led the way down the back stairs to the stone-floored Art Department. The former kitchen had been converted into the main art room several years before. Sculleries and pantries had been turned into workshops for woodwork, pottery and related subjects. There was a powerful smell that blended turpentine with wood-shavings and wet clay.

'It's in here.' Doncaster opened a door that gave on to a small office. 'This used to be the butler's pantry.' He switched on the light and nodded at a large, freestanding cupboard in one corner. 'Behind there.'

Bergerac glanced down. 'It's got castors. We'll pull it out.'

The cupboard was much lighter than it looked. He and Doncaster rolled it away from the wall.

Behind it they found a door. At some point it had been papered over to blend in with the walls. Later, someone had reopened it by sliding a knife along the cracks between door and jamb. The paper over the keyhole had also been cut away. He bent down: the key was in the lock on the other side.

'Look at that,' Doncaster said, drawing Bergerac's attention to the back of the cupboard.

A handle made of strong white plastic had been screwed into the wood. The back of the cupboard was festooned with cobwebs; but the handle itself was clean.

'Once the door's open,' Doncaster said excitedly, 'you just pull the cupboard back in place.'

Bergerac nodded. The idea was simple enough. The door itself had no handle. He pushed gently against it. There was no movement.

'We'll have to break it down,' he said, glancing over his shoulder. 'I take it you've no objection, sir?'

Upperwood shrugged. 'Would it matter if I had?'

'Go ahead, Sergeant,' Lady Wintersham said, assuming responsibility as though it belonged to her by divine right. 'But I warn you, you'll find nothing but rats down there.'

'I'll get a hammer and chisel from the carpentry shop,' Doncaster said. 'I don't think we've got a sledgehammer here. Or maybe a crowbar?'

The young teacher, Bergerac realized with a touch of bitterness, was enjoying himself. Life at Edward College must be relatively dull if you were used to the Royal Marines.

'Pity,' McCann muttered. 'It's going to make an awful lot of noise. Assuming that there's someone down there to hear.'

Doncaster returned, armed with a hammer and a big chisel.

'Smash through the panel above the lock,' Bergerac said. 'Then turn the key.'

The wood was too old and thin to offer much resistance. The chisel was through on the second blow. Doncaster tugged it out. There was a light on the other side.

172

He hammered in the chisel once more. The hole grew larger. But the light beyond had vanished.

'Damn,' Bergerac said. 'Has anyone got a torch?'

Doncaster and Goddard both had the ones they had used for the patrol. Bergerac snatched Goddard's. Apart from the hammer blows and splintering wood, the office was silent. Everyone was straining to catch the sound of movement beyond the door.

At last the hole was large enough for Doncaster to insert his hand. There was a click as the lock shot back. Doncaster's wrist was red with blood; he had scratched it on the jagged edge of the wood. He pushed the door backwards with a whoop of triumph.

Bergerac pushed him aside and plunged into the opening. There was a switch on the righthand side; he tried it, but nothing happened. By the light of the torch, he saw a flight of stone steps leading downwards to a stone-flagged floor that glistened with patches of damp.

He paused halfway down the steps. 'Wintersham!'

His voice echoed round the cellars. There was no answer.

A jump took him down to the ground. By the light of the torch he saw a long corridor that stretched towards the front of the house. The partition walls were of unplastered brick covered with discoloured and flaking whitewash. Doorways opened off both sides of the corridor. He flashed his torch into the nearest one. The beam flickered over a rusting bicycle with no front wheel, a pile of paint tins and a line of dusty bottles. Something scuttled away from the light. Whatever it was, it wasn't human.

Doncaster was the next down the stairs, waving his torch and giving off a strong smell of whisky and excitement.

'You and Goddard do the lefthand side,' Bergerac said. He glanced upwards. A familiar figure was shambling down the stairs behind Goddard. 'Doug, you come with me.' He raised his voice: 'And you two,' he barked at Lady Winter-sham and Upperwood, 'can stay exactly where you are.'

The search was methodical, thorough and infuriatingly slow. The place was a maze. Some cellars connected with their neighbours on either side of the passage; others gave on to further cellars behind them. They were filled with generations of rubbish – from empty, worm-eaten wine-racks to piles of unwanted textbooks. There were plenty of potential hiding places.

None of the individual cellars had electric light. The only socket was halfway down the corridor. Underneath it, McCann found a smashed lightbulb. The socket was still slightly warm too touch.

They worked slowly along the corridor, keeping in touch by shouts. Once Lady Wintersham screamed; but it proved to be a false alarm. She had seen a rat.

In one room Bergerac found an air vent that led upwards to a rusting grating. It was partly concealed by a gigantic oil painting, nearly six feet square, which was leaning against the wall. The picture seemed to depict – it was difficult to be sure because of the film of dirt that covered it – St Francis in the act of feeding a small menagerie of improbable animals. Above the grating were three distant stars. Below it, the dingy whitewash of the shaft was scuffed and scraped. He shone his torch to the ground. A sprinkling of fresh earth was scattered on the flags immediately below the shaft.

McCann whispered, 'Listen.'

Someone was snoring softly, just on the edge of their range of hearing. It should have been such a homely sound. In this place it was sinister.

McCann quickly checked the next cellar. 'It's not there. It's coming from here.'

Bergerac wrapped both hands round the frame of the picture and pulled. It fell forwards and crashed to the floor, sending up a cloud of dust. Behind it was another doorway. The torch's beam picked out a pair of legs encased in tight jeans.

In one corner of the little room, Rose Wintersham was lying on her front, breathing heavily. A half-bottle of Smirnoff vodka was standing on the floor, a few inches away from her hand. The torch glinted on a pill bottle, half-concealed by her outstretched arm. Bergerac scooped it up.

'Seconal,' he said. 'Lady Wintersham's prescription.'

McCann glanced at the bottle. 'Dear God.' For once there was no trace of hesitation in his speech. 'And she's been drinking.'

Bergerac nodded.

'Get Fender,' McCann said. 'He'll need a stomach pump. And lay on an ambulance . . .'

Bergerac was already moving. As he left he thought he heard McCann say something else.

'. . . or a hearse.'

CHAPTER
15

Barney Crozier was unshaven and angry.

'What a cock-up,' was the first thing he said to Bergerac when they were alone. 'This is what comes of trying to run the Bureau and CID in double harness.'

They were standing in the bursar's office during what felt like a lull in the storm. Lady Wintersham, trailing clouds of outrage, had just left with her daughter and Dr Fender in the ambulance that had been intended for Kim, who was still downstairs with Debby. Despite her maternal anxiety, Lady Wintersham had found time to lecture Crozier on his handling of the case, while simultaneously commandeering the ambulance; she was a woman of many parts.

'This'll look great,' Crozier went on bitterly. 'A teenage suicide bid, possibly brought on by police harassment.'

'Is that what she told you?' Bergerac was so suprised that he was temporarily speechless.

'Not just that: she also claims that the drugs and gloves were planted in Rose's room.'

'Come off it,' Bergerac said, remembering that Crozier had not yet been fully briefed. 'We've got Gunter's evidence that Rose was his biggest customer.'

'What about the suicide?' Crozier asked more cheerfully.

'No way. Someone must have been with Rose in the cellar. She wasn't capable of pulling out the lightbulb just before we got in. Plus there's the fact that it looks like someone made a hurried exit out of that grating. But if we hadn't got there in time, it might well have looked like suicide.'

Crozier looked at his watch. 'Make it snappy, Jim – we're needed downstairs. You still think it was Marcus Wintersham with the girl? Why?'

Bergerac leant against the desk. 'It starts with Poolstock and the murder of Yves on Thursday. Poolstock told me that he worked all morning at Heartland House. The study window overlooks the private gate to Mont Desir. When I asked him if he'd seen anyone, he said no, only the family, or words to that effect. But Lady Wintersham was still in London then, and Marcus said he spent all morning working in the coach-house; he made a point of stressing that he was inside, all the time. The only answer that fits is that Poolstock saw Marcus, and Marcus was lying. *But Poolstock didn't realize the significance of what he'd seen.*'

'It's hearsay now,' Crozier said dismissively, moving towards the door.

'Wait – there's more. Debby and Marcus met Poolstock this morning, and Poolstock made some remark about Marcus's leather camera case – mentioned seeing him with a metal one. Dodmarsh had a metal camera case, too, remember. It was then that Marcus must have realized that Poolstock had seen him. A few hours later, Poolstock has a fatal fall. Rather clever, for an improvisation: even if we'd realized it wasn't an accident, the Prankster would have seemed the obvious culprit.'

'It's plausible, I suppose. Though it's beyond me why someone like Wintersham should get involved with hard porn. In any case, all you've got is a theory. We need more evidence.'

'We need Marcus Wintersham,' Bergerac pointed out. 'The very fact we can't find him is suggestive.'

There was a knock on the door. One of McCann's DCs stuck his head into the room.

'Sorry to interrupt, sir. There's still no sign of Mr Wintersham. Sergeant McCann wants to know if you'll be needing him.'

'I'll come and see him,' Crozier said. As he was leaving, he said over his shoulder, 'And why the hell should he want to kill Rose?'

'Because she found the snuff movie that Charlie Hungerford got.'

'But how could Wintersham know that?'

'Debby told him this afternoon. The odds are that Rose found it at the coach-house. Did you know she has a history of petty thieving? That's what Debby told me just now. The important thing is that Rose could link him with the tape. Marcus must have realized then that he had to kill her. Another point is that only he and Rose had easy access to the Seconal.'

Crozier paused at the head of stairs. 'I grant you it all fits together. But you've got nothing that would convince a jury.'

'We will have if Rose talks.'

'*If* she talks,' Crozier said grimly. '*If* she recovers.'

'I'm not going to wait any longer,' Debby said. 'I'm going to drive Kim to hospital myself.'

'I don't *need* to go to hospital,' Kim said, 'I've only got a headache now.'

'You're going to hospital,' Akbar said flatly. He was sitting beside the sofa on which Kim was lying, with her head propped up on a couple of pillows. 'And I'm coming with you to hold your hand.'

To Debby's surprise, Kim made no further objection. At that moment Bergerac and Crozier came down the stairs. Bergerac agreed with them: the sooner Kim got to hospital, the better.

The Mercedes was where Debby had left it, just outside

the front door, with the keys still in the ignition. Bergerac and Akbar carried her to the car and settled her in the front passenger seat, whose back was as near to horizontal as it would go. Akbar clambered into the rear of the car.

'Good luck,' Bergerac said quietly. 'I've radioed down to the gate – they'll let you through at once.'

'Jim?' Debby paused, biting her lower lip. 'You think Marcus is involved?'

He nodded. 'I'm sorry. I really am.'

She bit her lip harder, to prevent herself from crying. Not in front of Jim.

'But what's happened to him?'

'We think he's still in the grounds somewhere. We've got the place sealed up, and we're putting out a general alert.'

For Marcus? There must be some sort of mistake.

'I'll phone you from the hospital,' she said calmly, 'when there's any news.'

'I'll come myself, as soon as I can.'

He went back to the house – back to the hunt for Marcus. Debby watched him. Over the years she had accumulated plenty of grudges against Bergerac, but there was one thing to be said for him: he took his responsibilities towards Kim seriously.

'Mum?' Kim said in a weak voice. 'I'm cold.'

'I'll get you something.'

Debby took the keys out of the ignition and went round to the boot. She made a point of keeping an old duffel coat there, since the time she had broken down in the depths of Northumberland one winter. She moved almost in a daze – her mind was full to overflowing with the memory of what had happened a few short hours before.

'Will you marry me?' Marcus said as they lay at peace in the big bed. 'Take me warts and all?'

'Yes,' she said, 'of course I will. From where I am, I can't even see any warts.'

'*You will, my love. You will.*'

'*It doesn't matter . . .*'

For a few seconds, she stood by the boot of the car, the keys dangling from her hand and the tears running down her face. Now, for just this instant, there was no one to see them. This evening she had wept with joy, for something found that she had thought was lost for ever. Now she wept because she had lost it again.

Her vision blurred, distorting the car in front of her. She dug in her pocket for a tissue. This wouldn't do. There was no time for self-pity. Kim needed her. She dabbed her eyes, and the car returned to normal. She pushed the key in the lock.

And stopped.

The car wasn't normal, not quite. The lid of the boot was fractionally out of true.

She knew what it was: the catch that held the lid was not engaged. But it should have been, because she had slammed it herself when she got back home this evening.

'*I've radioed down to the gate – they'll let you through at once.*'

So she had a choice. Between a lover and an ex-husband. Between a new life and the old one. Between inclination on the one hand and that hard, masculine virtue they called duty on the other. A couple of seconds became an eternity of indecision. Bergerac hadn't had time to say what Marcus was supposed to have done. Did it really matter? Once Kim was safe in hospital, anything could happen. There was Dad's boat, waiting for them at the marina. She had money of her own. There must be somewhere in the world where they could go and be happy. Just this once, she had a chance to please herself. And Marcus needed her: that was the sweetest pleasure of all.

Warts and all? Well, why not?

The front door opened. Bergerac and Crozier were on the steps.

In the car, Kim moaned faintly.

That was why.

Debby put both hands on the lid of the boot and pushed downwards. There was some resistance, as if someone was pushing against the other side. But she had far more leverage. The lock on the boot engaged itself with a faint, well-oiled click.

'Jim,' she said. Her eyes were dry. 'You'd better come over here.'

CHAPTER
16

'Do you think it'll work?' Jenny Godly said. 'She may be beyond caring.'

'It's worth a try.'

Bergerac slowed for a junction. Jenny glanced at his profile, which looked as stern and unforgiving as the weather. No reassurance there. The rain drummed down on the windscreen. The wipers were having difficulty in coping. So was she.

'It feels . . .'

'What?' he said.

'Immoral, I suppose. Hitting someone when they're down.'

'She's not down – just a bit bruised. It won't last.'

They drove through the underpass beneath Fort Regent. There was little traffic, even by the usual Sunday morning standards of St Helier; the weather was keeping people indoors. In the course of the last week, they seemed to have moved directly from summer to winter, without a break for autumn.

'Lady Wintersham fought it, the whole way,' Bergerac said abruptly. 'And she didn't lose, either. Why do you think there's been so little in the press? Why do you think Rose has been carted off to a Swiss sanatorium instead of standing trial? Lady Wintersham's even used her friends – including Hungerford, by the way – to pull strings in the States Police: we play ball, and they don't amalgamate the

Bureau with CID. We're dropping charges against Rose. So's the school. It makes me sick.'

Jenny had never heard such bitterness in his voice. She tried to turn the conversation to something less controversial.

'So Rose admitted being the Prankster?'

'Oh, yes – said it was to get back at her mother.' He hesitated, then added: 'Did you know that Marcus's father died insane?'

'No. But it explains quite a lot.'

'We've got Marcus, at least,' Bergerac said. 'Though he won't get what he deserves because he's turning Queen's Evidence. Part of the deal is that we pretend to believe him when he says he didn't kill Poolstock or Yves.'

'Should you be telling me all this?'

'No. But I'm going to.' He grinned suddenly at her. 'If I don't tell someone, I'll explode. Besides, you're a historian. You can write down the truth for future generations.'

She was curious, despite her misgivings. 'You can start by telling me why. Everyone said that Marcus was rich.'

'He inherited something like two million quid from his father. But he's a compulsive gambler – horses, mainly. Two or three years ago, he was near rock-bottom. He had to find some way of keeping himself in the manner to which he was accustomed.'

'But I thought his house was practically dripping with Expressionist art. Couldn't he sell some of it?'

'He did. Privately, of course, and after he'd had some copies made. Then he lost the proceeds on the Cheltenham Gold Cup. Dodmarsh was a racing crony, so he knew the score. When he needed an agent on Jersey, Marcus was the obvious choice. Rich, well-respected and influential. He was the perfect cut-out between Dodmarsh the distributor on the British mainland and Akbar's cousin in Paris, who was the buyer for the operation.'

They had already reached Gorey. Jenny wished that Bergerac would slow down. She was not looking forward to the approaching interview.

'They used Akbar as the courier between Paris and here,' Bergerac went on relentlessly. 'The boy knew nothing about it, of course – he was just the expendable fall-guy if customs got too curious. He left the tapes at a one-room office in St Helier, which Dodmarsh rented for Marcus, just for that purpose. Marcus picked them up and met Dodmarsh or his representative at Mont Desir. Neat idea – Marcus could get in and out without anyone knowing; and Dodmarsh or whoever was just one more tourist. They found a quiet place – like the Jersey Rose tableau – and just swapped camera cases. Money in one, tapes in the other. Yves was just unlucky: he witnessed the rendezvous, and he knew both men by sight.'

'Which of them killed him?'

'Dodmarsh says Marcus. Marcus says Dodmarsh. Take your pick. Then, last Sunday, Marcus realized that both Poolstock and Rose were dangerous to him. So there was only one solution.'

Jenny shivered.

'My ex-wife,' Bergerac said harshly, 'was in love with him. And now she's one of the walking wounded. She didn't deserve that. Damn it, I even liked the man myself. Do you know, that's the worst thing about it – I actually *liked* him.'

They passed the gates of Edward College, where Nigel Upperwood was learning to cope with the simultaneous losses of his wife, his bursar, his self-respect and the good reputation of his school.

In front of them, Mont Desir sprawled on its rainswept headland, empty of tourists and criminals, curators and corpses. It was closed for the winter. Only the ghosts were left.

Bergerac slowed for the turn into the drive of Heartland House.

'What did you say when you phoned her?' Jenny said.

'That a friend and I wanted to call on urgent family business that couldn't be mentioned over the phone. Her family.'

The Triumph Roadster dawdled up the winding drive among the dripping rhododendrons and fuchsias.

'She deserves it, love,' Bergerac said softly. 'Quite apart from anything else, she's a ruthless, domineering woman who needs to learn that she can't always have her own way.'

Jenny glanced at him. 'I'd say your own ruthlessness rating isn't bad, either.'

'It's in a good cause.'

'Maybe, but . . .' Her voice tailed away. They had been through this before. As far as Bergerac was concerned, the argument was over. Or, to be more precise, he had never really understood that there was an argument in the first place.

He parked as near to the front door as he could get. They ran through the rain to the shelter of the porch. Muddy water splashed against Jenny's tights and shoes.

This time a maid answered the door.

'Lady Wintersham's expecting us,' Bergerac said.

The maid showed them into the L-shaped drawing room. Lady Wintersham, dressed in black, was sitting in a wing armchair by the fire. Her eyebrows rose when she saw Jenny.

'Dr Godly! I didn't expect to see you here. A problem at the museum?'

'Not exactly.' Jenny glanced at the mantelpiece with its photograph of Edward VII.

'Do sit down,' Lady Wintersham said automatically. She

dismissed the maid without offering her guests a drink. 'Now, how can I help you?'

It was superb, Jenny thought: their hostess had a nephew in jail, her daughter in a sanatorium and a cartload of scandal to cope with; but the *grande dame* manner was intact.

'I must ask you to be brief,' Lady Wintersham went on. 'I have a luncheon engagement.' She glanced at Bergerac. 'Something about my family, I think you said?'

'First I have a request. Dr Godly tells me that there is statutory provision for Foundation Scholarships at Edward College?'

She frowned. 'That is correct. My grandmother believed in helping the people to help themselves. But – '

'"To be appointed at the discretion of the governors,"' Jenny quoted. 'I looked up the school's charter. Under statute you also have the power to extend the scholarships to include expenses at university.'

'The school's constitution does include such a provision,' Lady Wintersham agreed cautiously. 'However, I fail to see why you should want to discuss the terms of the foundation with me on a Sunday morning.'

Bergerac said, 'We would like you to recommend that a Foundation Scholarship be granted to Akbar Farzanah; to be extended, if he wishes, to support him through medical school.'

'Don't be absurd.'

'The boy's money was embezzled by his guardian, your nephew's associate,' Bergerac said. 'The French police have arrested the man, but the money's salted away, out of their reach. At the end of this term, Akbar will be out on his ear because he can't pay his fees. I think a scholarship would be a fine gesture on the part of the governors.' His face was deadpan. He added, softly, 'Good for the image, even.'

She shrugged her plump, expensively covered shoulders.

186

'It's not our responsibility.' She looked directly at Jenny, who resisted the temptation to cower away from the glare. A bullying note crept into her voice. 'What exactly are you doing with this man, Dr Godly?'

The change in tone stiffened Jenny's resolution. The implication was that Dr Godly, as an employee of the Historical Trust, existed to do the bidding of the trustees in the shape of Lady Wintersham.

'You could say I'm the hired muscle.'

'Is that a colloquialism? I'm afraid I do not understand.'

'We're proposing a deal, Lady Wintersham,' Jenny said as calmly as she could manage. It was easier once she had started. 'A scholarship for Akbar on your side, in return for an undertaking not to write a biography of the Jersey Rose on ours.'

'A biography? What *are* you talking about?'

'We both know that that man' – Jenny nodded towards the photograph – 'is no more your ancestor than he's mine. The Jersey Rose was a conwoman. I can make out an excellent *prima facie* case without even thinking about it. If I really dig into it, I doubt if I'd have much trouble in proving the point.'

It's madness, Jenny thought desperately. *I'm risking my job for the sake of Jim Bergerac's blue eyes. And not just my job. I need my head examined.*

The silence gave no answers. Lady Wintersham sat back in her chair, looking at neither of her guests. She could certainly make Jenny's position at the Museum untenable, even if she couldn't hope successfully to accuse them of blackmail. And that was what it was, Jenny realized with a shock: blackmail, however it was disguised as Jim Bergerac's private system for punishing the wicked and supporting the weak.

Lady Wintersham stirred. 'Akbar Farzanah, you said?' Her voice was assured as ever. It was as though the part of the conversation that had dealt with the Jersey Rose no longer existed. 'On second thoughts, you may have a point. He's a deserving case, and it would be a humanitarian gesture. After all, Edward College is a charitable body.'

'Good,' Bergerac said, rising to his feet. 'We'll look forward to hearing the announcement. Thank you for seeing us, Lady Wintersham.'

A few seconds later, he and Jenny were back in the porch. It was still pelting with rain. Mont Desir looked as though it was about to dissolve.

They made a run for the car. Jenny sat in the passenger seat, flicking water from her skirt.

'You deserve the best lunch money can buy,' Bergerac said. 'I've booked a table at the Coq d'Or.'

Jenny shook her head listlessly. She felt drained – partly by the interview, and partly because the argument in her head had reached its uncomfortable conclusion.

Like Lady Wintersham, he thinks the end justified the means. They're two of a kind, under the skin.

'I want to go home,' she said. 'Alone.'

FOR THE BEST IN PAPERBACKS, LOOK FOR THE

In every corner of the world, on every subject under the sun, Penguin represents quality and variety – the very best in publishing today.

For complete information about books available from Penguin – including Pelicans, Puffins, Peregrines and Penguin Classics – and how to order them, write to us at the appropriate address below. Please note that for copyright reasons the selection of books varies from country to country.

In the United Kingdom: For a complete list of books available from Penguin in the U.K., please write to *Dept E.P., Penguin Books Ltd, Harmondsworth, Middlesex, UB7 0DA*

In the United States: For a complete list of books available from Penguin in the U.S., please write to *Dept BA, Penguin, 299 Murray Hill Parkway, East Rutherford, New Jersey 07073*

In Canada: For a complete list of books available from Penguin in Canada, please write to *Penguin Books Canada Ltd, 2801 John Street, Markham, Ontario L3R 1B4*

In Australia: For a complete list of books available from Penguin in Australia, please write to the *Marketing Department, Penguin Books Australia Ltd, P.O. Box 257, Ringwood, Victoria 3134*

In New Zealand: For a complete list of books available from Penguin in New Zealand, please write to the *Marketing Department, Penguin Books (NZ) Ltd, Private Bag, Takapuna, Auckland 9*

In India: For a complete list of books available from Penguin, please write to *Penguin Overseas Ltd, 706 Eros Apartments, 56 Nehru Place, New Delhi, 110019*

In Holland: For a complete list of books available from Penguin in Holland, please write to *Penguin Books Nederland B.V., Postbus 195, NL–1380AD Weesp, Netherlands*

In Germany: For a complete list of books available from Penguin, please write to *Penguin Books Ltd, Friedrichstrasse 10 – 12, D–6000 Frankfurt Main 1, Federal Republic of Germany*

In Spain: For a complete list of books available from Penguin in Spain, please write to *Longman Penguin España, Calle San Nicolas 15, E–28013 Madrid, Spain*

PENGUIN BESTSELLERS

Is That It? Bob Geldof with Paul Vallely

The autobiography of one of today's most controversial figures. 'He has become a folk hero whom politicians cannot afford to ignore. And he has shown that simple moral outrage can be a force for good' – *Daily Telegraph*. 'It's terrific . . . everyone over thirteen should read it' – *Standard*

Niccolò Rising Dorothy Dunnett

The first of a new series of historical novels by the author of the world-famous *Lymond* series. Adventure, high romance and the dangerous glitter of fifteenth-century Europe abound in this magnificent story of the House of Charetty and the disarming, mysterious genius who exploits all its members.

The World, the Flesh and the Devil Reay Tannahill

'A bewitching blend of history and passion. A MUST' – *Daily Mail*. A superb novel in a great tradition. 'Excellent' – *The Times*

Perfume: The Story of a Murderer Patrick Süskind

It was after his first murder that Grenouille knew he was a genius. He was to become the greatest perfumer of all time, for he possessed the power to distil the very essence of love itself. 'Witty, stylish and ferociously absorbing . . . menace conveyed with all the power of the writer's elegant unease' – *Observer*

The Old Devils Kingsley Amis

Winner of the 1986 Booker Prize
'Vintage Kingsley Amis, 50 per cent pure alcohol with splashes of sad savagery' – *The Times*. The highly comic novel about Alun Weaver and his wife's return to their Celtic roots. 'Crackling with marvellous Taff comedy . . . this is probably Mr Amis's best book since *Lucky Jim*' – *Guardian*

PENGUIN BESTSELLERS

Cat Chaser   Elmore Leonard

'*Cat Chaser* really moves' – *The New York Times Book Review*. 'Elmore Leonard gets so much mileage out of his plot that just when you think one is cruising to a stop, it picks up speed for a few more twists and turns' – *Washington Post*.

Men and Angels   Mary Gordon

A rich, astonishing novel of the limits of human and divine love.' A domestic drama of morals with a horrifying climax . . . compellingly readable' – *Sunday Times*. 'A brilliant study of the insatiable demands of the unlovable' – *Standard*

The Mosquito Coast   Paul Theroux

Detesting twentieth century America, Allie Fox takes his family to live in the Honduran jungle. 'Imagine the Swiss Family Robinson gone mad, and you will have some idea of what is in store . . . Theroux's best novel yet' – *Sunday Times* (Now a powerful film.)

The King's Garden   Fanny Deschamps

In a story which ranges from the opulent corruption of Louis XV's court to the storms and dangers of life on the high seas, Jeanne pursues her happiness and the goal of true love with all the determination and his spirits of one born to succeed . . .

Let No Man Divide   Elizabeth Kary

Set against the turmoil of the American Civil War, *Let No Man Divide* tells of Leigh Pemberton's desire to nurse the wounded and live an independent life, and her secret yearning for Hayes Bannister, the man who has saved her life and taken her breath away.

Castaway Lucy Irvine

'A savagely self-searching tale . . . she is a born writer as well as a ruthlessly talented survivor' – *Observer*. 'Fascinating' – *Daily Mail*. 'Remarkable . . . such dreams as stuff is made of' – *Financial Times*

Runaway Lucy Irvine

Not a sequel, but the story of Lucy Irvine's life *before* she became a castaway. Witty, courageous and sensational, it is a story you won't forget. 'A searing account . . . raw and unflinching honesty' – *Daily Express*. 'A genuine and courageous work of autobiography' – *Today*

The Adventures of Goodnight and Loving Leslie Thomas

Sometimes touching, sometimes hilarious, sometimes alarming, the adventures of George Goodnight represent a quest for excitement and love. 'A constant pleasure. Leslie Thomas is to the contemporary novel what Alan Ayckborn is to the Theatre: a wry humorist with the rare ability to make his audience feel as well as laugh' – *Sunday Telegraph*

Wideacre Philippa Gregory

Beatrice Lacey is one of the most passionate and compelling heroines ever created. There burns in Beatrice one overwhelming obsession – to possess Wideacre, her family's ancestral home, and to achieve her aim she will risk everything; reputation, incest, even murder.

A Dark and Distant Shore Reay Tannahill

'An absorbing saga spanning a century of love affairs, hatred and high-points of Victorian history' – *Daily Express*. 'Enthralling . . . a marvellous blend of *Gone with the Wind* and *The Thorn Birds*. You will enjoy every page' – *Daily Mirror*